I0641381

# Blanche Baughan

## SELECTED WRITINGS

edited by

Damian Love

EREWHON
PRESS

Published by Erewhon Press 2015

Erewhon Press
23/5 Eva Street
Wellington 6011

ISBN 978-0-473-30943-5

Typeset in Minion Pro 10.5/13

# SELECTED WRITINGS

BLANCHE BAUGHAN (1870–1958) was one of the most spirited figures among New Zealand's literary pioneers. Born in Surrey, she earned a first in Classics at Royal Holloway College, London, before spending much of the 1890s engaged in social work in the East End slums. Her first collection, *Verses* (1898), while showing little originality, announced a poet with a good ear and promising rhythmic gift. After emigrating to New Zealand in 1900, settling eventually in Banks Peninsula, she pursued a literary career in earnest, publishing her two most substantial verse collections, *Reuben* (1903) and *Shingle-Short* (1908). Her collection of prose stories, *Brown Bread from a Colonial Oven* (1912), offered some sprightly sketches of typical lives in the settler period. Her most popular success was her series of journalistic essays documenting her extensive travels around many of the country's most remarkable landscapes, collected as *Studies in New Zealand Scenery* (1916), a book that often displays her exceptional gusto and relish for detail. Baughan's literary energy petered out with the disappointing verse collection *Poems from the Port Hills* (1923), and for the rest of her life she turned to social work, for which she was awarded the King George V Jubilee Medal in 1935. In particular she made a significant contribution to prison reform in New Zealand. Her book *People in Prison* (1936) spoke out against a backward and callous penal system and provided lively compassionate portraits of some the inmates she befriended.

# Contents

# *Introduction*

Blanche Edith Baughan, a pioneer by nature, was the first woman to write significant poetry in New Zealand.

Born in 1870 in Surrey, England, she was among the earliest women to attend Royal Holloway College in London and its first student of all to gain a first-class degree in Classics. Her vocation for social work emerged soon after graduation: she spent much of the 1890s working in the slums of east London. She also had serious literary aspirations, and published her first collection, *Verses*, in 1898. In 1900 she travelled to New Zealand, settling by 1902 in the little Banks Peninsula community of Chorlton. Over the next decade she pursued a writing career, producing her two most substantial verse collections, *Reuben* (1903) and *Shingle-Short* (1908), as well as a book of prose stories, *Brown Bread from a Colonial Oven* (1912). Her essay on the Milford Track, 'The Finest Walk in the World' (1908), led over the next few years to a series of popular tramping sketches, collected in 1916 as *Studies in New Zealand Scenery*. But her poetic energy waned, and her last poems, written before the First World War and published in 1923 as *Poems from the Port Hills*, are uniformly poor.

Baughan herself was quick to realize her muse had deserted her. After extensive travels between 1915 and 1920, including a trip to India in pursuit of Vedanta enlightenment, she devoted herself increasingly to social work. In 1924 she helped found the New Zealand branch of the Howard League for Penal Reform. Baughan studied prison conditions closely, acted as official visitor at Addington Reformatory for Women in Christchurch, and used her own home and income to shelter and assist ex-prisoners and other misfits. Her controversially received book *People in Prison* (1936) offered lively, sympathetic portraits of inmates and a scathing indictment of the retrograde

stupidity of the New Zealand penal system. In 1935 she was awarded
the King George V Jubilee Medal for her social work.

Blanche Baughan died in Akaroa on 20 August 1958.

She is best remembered now for a handful of poems that rise
convincingly above tired 'poetic' diction, among which 'The Old
Place' is the most outstanding:

> So the last day's come at last, the close of my fifteen year—
> The end of the hope, an' the struggles, an' messes I've put in here.
> All of the shearings over, the final mustering done,—
> Eleven hundred an' fifty for the incoming man, near on.

Others had used ballad forms, colloquialisms and dropped aitches to
convey working-class experience or the life of a raw colony. Indeed
this resource had already become part of Victoriana and would con-
tinue to be worn threadbare for decades to come. Baughan's demotics
are, on the whole, no less ersatz than most such verse, but she had a
genuine rhythmic gift that at times lifts her monologues into dramatic
conviction. She never lacked enthusiasm, in any aspect of her life,
and her long loose lines are a successful vehicle for it, principally
because she rarely allows them to thud. Her deft handling may easily
be underappreciated—today's norms of technical accomplishment
in New Zealand verse have by no means eclipsed hers.

Her Achilles heel is, of course, sentimentality. She had the misfortune to be a minor writer on the edge of a period in which even the
major ones were supine to that vice. What Dickens or Eliot may get
away with—and they don't always—will not last well in the works of
a Baughan or a Coventry Patmore. Some of her stories and poems,
not collected here, are beyond export from the age of the Victorian
parlour, and even her more durable writing tends to flirt heavily
with its domestic pieties. Elizabeth's monologue from *The Paddock*,
for instance, has an undeniable moral cosiness, although it is also
a plausible enough account of typical hardships overcome, and if it
comes off, it is because the verse is skilfully wrought.

Blanche Baughan can all too easily seem at first glance like a maiden aunt, brandishing oversized hats and philanthropic crusades, a figure too quaint these days to be invited out much. In truth, however, she devoted herself urgently and tirelessly to social justice, and was more open than most of us will ever be to the lives of society's down-and-outs. The visitor at Addington Reformatory offers a certain perspective on the creative writing seminar circuit. It is noteworthy, too, that in those days of supposed cultural cringe she tramped and sailed her way around more of New Zealand, and had a more intimate knowledge of its landscape, its flora and fauna, its rural communities than the vast majority of its current inhabitants.

We cannot choose our founding fathers, or our founding mothers either. If we could, we would choose a more cogent author than Baughan. But she is what we have, and recognizing the felicities in her minor verse may help save us from overestimating the minor verse of our own day. Appreciating the verve encased in her Edwardian journalism may help us discern the timebound limitations of our own journalistic output. And her sometimes critical patriotism may still shed light on a few of our vanities.

*Damian Love*
*Wellington 2014*

# PART I

*Selected Poems*

from *Verses* (1898)

## Death-in-Life

Awhile ago I lay down in this place,
    Hard by the summit of a heathery hill.
    The Autumn afternoon was very still,
All things seem'd melting into sunny space.
I lay long, looking in the sky's dear face,
    Wearing my heart away with prayers, until
    Nature releas'd me from my weary will,
Gave me sweet Death-in-Life.

                                O sovereign grace!
Gone is the misty question, 'What am I?'
    No part of me but in the sunlight shares.
I am become a morsel of blue sky,
    A breath among the slowly-sauntering airs,
A tuft of heather, rooted where I lie—
    Anything, save a creature that hath cares!

## Trafalgar Square

Strong isle of stillness 'mid a roaring sea!
    Like some great Queen thy solitude doth stand,
    Deigning with quiet majesty and grand
To front these wild waves of Humanity.
How proud a privilege is granted thee!
    All round thou see'st the mighty flood expand,

Hear'st its hoarse voice of thunderous command,
Know'st all its power; yet from that power art free!

Man's joy, Man's woe, his hunger and his wealth,
    For ever art thou contemplating these;
Yet still thy fountains fill the air with health,
    Above the glaring pavement dream thy trees.
—Could but my soul, herself as free from strife,
As fully face each fact of human life!

## Barbara

### I

I saw three ships go sailing,
    And two I've seen come back;
A ship of war, and a merchant ship,—
    And the third was a fisher-smack.

The first is back with glory,
    The next with treasure stor'd.—
But the little smack, she'll ne'er be back,
    That had my love aboard.

### II

Seven riding-lights but now;
    Now, only three.
And still creeps the sheeted fog
    Across the numb sea.

A night's fog for the fisher-boats,
    A night's fog for the sea—
Night on night, day on day
    A life's fog for me.

III

North I turn, but never his face I find;
    South,—but it is not there!
Night cannot lull my sorrow asleep, nor dawn
    Awaken my despair.

But, oft-times, 'twixt the rim of the dying day,
    And the rim of the darkening sea,
Hope spies the pearly gleam of that far-off Sail,
    Will give him back to me!


## *Pebbles*

Pebbles, pebbles by the sea,
Is it, I wonder, better to be
Snatch'd away by the hurrying waves,
Swallow'd down to the rolling caves,
Where the mad water wrestles and raves:
Dash'd upon rocks, champ'd amid foam,
    Toss'd and turn'd,
    Trampled and churn'd,
Spued out at last on the self-same shore,
Flung back awhile to the self-same home,
—Not the same pebbles as before!
But smooth'd and rounded and jewel bright,
A line of laughter, a dance of light,
The shore's glory, the sun's delight:

Or is it better, high and dry
Out of the great sea's reach to lie?
    Night by night and day by day
    From the wild waves hid away:
    On a landward ledge to stay,
Never fretted, jostled, hurl'd

With a jarring crash,
And a sharp splash,
From the surety and the peace
Of your never-changing world:
Comfortable, safe, at ease:
—Sore to the eye, sharp to the hand,
Stark upon the weary strand
Like bleach'd bones in an unslaked land?

# from *Reuben and Other Poems* (1903)

## *The Two Ships*

(To G. H. C. S.)

I dream'd I stood on some advanced cliff
Heading the harbourage of Heaven, and watch'd,
From out the open deep, their voyage done,
Ships making port; and these I knew for souls,
Coming from earthly travel home to God,
But in the very guise of ships they came;
Diverse in build, of varying speed, and size
Unequal; and among them, as I look'd,
Chiefly conspicuous, two.

                The first swam in,
Beauty incarnate! From the distant blue
Stately emerging, gliding gradual on,
Her visionary towers of swelling snow,
Aerial, azure-spaced, offended not
That crystal atmosphere, shamed not one beam
Of that celestial light. And closer come,
No flaw belittled, no neglect belied
That majesty of mien, but burnish'd shone
Her tapering spars, and glittering-bright her trucks.
Her hull, from cleaving stem to sheering stern,
In gracious lines all freshly-glancing ran,
And in her well-trimmed sails, her ropes all taut,
Her rigging well set-up and rattled down,
Her order'd decks and steady steering, lay
Proof of a full and unscathed company.

How otherwise the other! Stoutly built,
With engines to give certainty and speed,
She sagg'd and labour'd in that halcyon calm,
Her steam deficient, all her pumps at work,
And hardly made her haven, staggering in
It seem'd at hazard, with that wavering wake.
Nearer, sea-crusted weary sides she show'd,
Dented and scored, and o'er the bow a sail
Suck'd in to stop some gash—and, even so,
Down by the head she was. Her davits yawn'd
Boatless; and of enfeebled strength and stores
Exhausted spoke the details of her gear,
Where all not rust was rotten. Beggarly,
Disabled, unseaworthy, in she crept
Like refuse in the other's regal wake,
And, 'mid that home of pure perennial joy,
Stank of old sorrows.

                Watching both, 'What mirth,
What exultation new!' I said, 'awaits
The happy Overseers angelical,
When at her berth arrived yon faultless ship
They scan, and, making true report to Him
That builded her and owns, perceive His smile,
But this poor wreck—for other destinies
Launch'd, by her make,—at such her home-return
What but a shamefaced pity can they feel,
And disappointment He?'

                    Then answer'd one:
'Thou seest the arrival. Hast thou watch'd the voyage?
Happy the ship with cargo well bestow'd
At starting, and in sailing a fair wind:
'Twixt port and port her course set clear, by coasts
Unperilous, o'er roomy waters calm.

But—storms outridden, scarce-escapèd reefs,
Freight slowly won at many a sunder'd port,
Painfully shipp'd and borne thro' many foes:
Collision suffer'd: and to long endure
The usage of the brine: and yet win home—
This asks for staunchness, strength and enterprise,
This courage claims, and seamanship exact.
And should it not bring honour?'

                        Hereupon,
The vessel I at first admired, I now
Despised, and 'How much happier,' I cried,
'More to be envied, much more glorious,
Nay, in the Builder's sight, how far more fair,
This crawling-in triumphant, than yon calm
Easy re-entry, unreproved, unproven!'

But he: 'Why wilt thou mete the more and less?
Each her due course obedient having sail'd,
Each her desired cargo faithful borne,
Delightful to the Heavenly Eye come both.'


## Young Hotspur

Farewell to you, gully and paddock and peak,
And you, lonely old *whare* aside of the creek!
Lonely and silent, you'll see me no more,
For I've finished with farming: I'm off to the war.

I have scored my last tally, I've done my last dip,
And, thank God, there's no crutching aboard of a ship.
No more of the yards and the race and the pen,
For I'm going—I'm going to live among *men*!

Who next on my stretcher his blanket will spread,
And curse this old oven for burning his bread?
Poor beggar! he'll stare at that map till he's sick of it,
Here—while, hurrah! *I* shall be in the thick of it.

Cushie, old woman, you'll feel a fresh hand,
And the dogs 'll get working they won't understand.
Ay, Roy and Rover, you'll miss me a bit;
Well, I don't care who misses, so long as I hit!

Last night I was hearing my mother looked sad,
And a face at the station's not overly glad.
But when fighting and fun have got hold of a man,
Why,—the women must manage the best way they can.

What's kisses, and comfort? The worth of a pin
When there's wrongs to be righted, and honours to win:
When the country is up, and they're calling from Home,
And you've long'd all your life for a bit of a roam!

And suppose, one fine evening, the old Cross up there
Down at me dead on some kopje should stare—
All right! I'll have met with some reason for breath;
Life I'll have tasted before I feed Death.

Here's the moon, Russet! Not much of a lamp,
And a dozen odd miles to pick back into camp.
Up! Good-bye, *whare* and paddock and all!
It's 'Hurrah for New Zealand, and down with Oom Paul!'


## The Old Place

So the last day's come at last, the close of my fifteen year—
The end of the hope, an' the struggles, an' messes I've put in here.
All of the shearings over, the final mustering done,—

Eleven hundred an' fifty for the incoming man, near on.
Over five thousand I drove 'em, mob by mob, down the coast;
Eleven-fifty in fifteen year… it isn't much of a boast.

Oh, it's a bad old place! Blown out o' your bed half the nights,
And in summer the grass burnt shiny an' bare as your hand, on the
    heights:
The creek dried up by November, and in May a thundering roar
That carries down toll o' your stock to salt 'em whole on the shore.
Clear'd I have, and I've clear'd an' clear'd, yet everywhere, slap in
    your face,
Briar, *tauhinu*, an' ruin!—God! it's a brute of a place.
… An' the house got burnt which I built, myself, with all that worry
    and pride;
Where the Missus was always homesick, and where she took fever,
    and died.

Yes, well! I'm leaving the place. Apples look red on that bough.
I set the slips with my own hand. Well—they're the other man's now.
The breezy bluff: an' the clover that smells so over the land,
Drowning the reek o' the rubbish, that plucks the profit out o' your
    hand:
That bit o' Bush paddock I fall'd myself, an' watched, each year, come
    clean
(Don't it look fresh in the tawny? A scrap of Old-Country green):
This air, all healthy with sun an' salt, an' bright with purity:
An' the glossy *karakas* there, twinkling to the big blue twinkling sea:
Ay, the broad blue sea beyond, an' the gem-clear cove below,
Where the boat I'll never handle again, sits rocking to and fro:
There's the last look to it all! an' now for the last upon
This room, where Hetty was born, an' my Mary died, an' John…

Well! I'm leaving the poor old place, and it cuts as keen as a knife;
The place that's broken my heart—the place where I've lived my life.

## from *Shingle-Short* (1908)

## *A Bush Section*

Logs, at the door, by the fence; logs, broadcast over the paddock;
Sprawling in motionless thousands away down the green of the gully,
Logs, grey-black. And the opposite rampart of ridges
Bristles against the sky, all the tawny, tumultuous landscape
Is stuck, and prickled, and spiked with the standing black and grey
   splinters,
Strewn, all over its hollows and hills, with the long, prone, grey-
   black logs.

   For along the paddock, and down the gully,
   Over the multitudinous ridges,
   Through valley and spur,
   Fire has been!
Ay, the Fire went through and the Bush has departed,
The green Bush departed, green Clearing is not yet come.
   'Tis a silent, skeleton world;
   Dead, and not yet re-born,
   Made, unmade, and scarcely as yet in the making;
   Ruin'd, forlorn, and blank.

At the little raw farm on the edge of the desolate hillside,
Perch'd on the brink, overlooking the desolate valley,
To-night, now the milking is finish'd, and all the calves fed,
The kindling all split, and the dishes all wash'd after supper:
Thorold von Reden, the last of a long line of nobles,
Little 'Thor Rayden', the twice-orphan'd son of a drunkard,
Dependent on strangers, the taciturn, grave ten-year-old,

Stands and looks from the garden of cabbage and larkspur, looks over
The one little stump-spotted rye-patch, so gratefully green,
Out, on this desert of logs, on this dead disconsolate ocean
Of billows arrested, of currents stay'd, that never awake and flow.
Day after day,
The hills stand out on the sky,
The splinters stand on the hills,
In the paddock the logs lie prone.
The prone logs never arise,
The erect ones never grow green,
Leaves never rustle, the birds went away with the Bush,—
There is no change, nothing stirs!
And to-night there is no change;
All is mute, monotonous, stark;
In the whole wide sweep round the low little hut of the settler
No life to be seen; nothing stirs.

    Yet, see! past the cow-bails,
      Down, deep in the gully,
    What glimmers? What silver
      Streaks the grey dusk?
'Tis the River, the River! Ah, gladly Thor thinks of the River,
His playmate, his comrade,
Down there all day,
All the long day, betwixt lumber and cumber,
Sparkling and singing;
Lively glancing, adventurously speeding,
Busy and bright as a needle in knitting
Running in, running out, running over and under
The logs that bridge it, the logs that block it,
The logs that helplessly trail in its waters,
The jamm'd-up jetsam, the rooted snags.
Twigs of *konini*, bronze leaf-boats of wineberry
Launch'd in the River, they also will run with it,
They cannot stop themselves, twisting and twirling

They too will keep running, away and away
Yes; for on runs the River, it presses, it passes
On—by the fence, by the bails, by the landslip, away down the gully,
On, ever onward and on!
The hills remain, the logs and the gully remain,
Changeless as ever, and still;
But the River changes, the River passes.
Nothing else stirring about it,
It stirs, it is quick, 'tis alive!
   'What is the River, the running River?
   Where does it come from?
   Where does it go?'
        Listen! Listen!...
Far away, down the voiceless valley,
Thro' league-long spaces of empty air,
A sound! as of thunder.
        Look! ah, look!
   Yonder, deep in the clear dark distance,
At the foot of the shaggy, snow-hooded ranges,—
   Out of the houseless and homeless country
   Suddenly issuing, eddying, volleying—
Smoke, bright smoke! Not the soft blue vapour
By day, in the paddock there, wreathing and wavering,
O'er the red spark well at work in the stumps:
Not the poor little misty pale pillar
Here straggling up, close at hand, from the crazy tin chimney:—
No! but an airy river of riches,
Irrepressibly billowing, volume on volume
Rolling, unrolling, tempestuously tossing,
Ah! like the glorious hair of some else-invisible Angel
Rushing splendidly forth in the darkness—
Gold! gold on the gloom!
... Floating, fleeing, flying...
Thor catches his breath... Ah, flown!

Gone! Yes, the torrent of glory,
The Voice and the Vision are gone—
For over the viaduct, out of the valley,
It is gone, the wonderful Train!
Gone, yet still going on: on: on! to the far-away township
(Ten miles off, down the track, and the mud of the metal-less roadway:
Seen, once at Christmas, and once on a fine summer Sunday:
Always a dream, with its dozens of passing people,
Its three beneficent stores)…
And past the township, and on!
—The hills and the gully remain;
One day is just like another;
In the paddock the logs lie still;
But the Train is not still; every evening it sparkles out, streams by
    and goes.
        'What is the Train, that it travels?
        Where does it come from?
        Where does it go?'

It is gone. And the evening deepens.
Darker the grey air grows.
From the black of the gully, the gleam of the River is gone.
Scarcely the ridges show to the sky-line,
Now, their disconsolate fringe;
But, bright to the deepening sky,
The Stars creep silently out.
'Oh, where do you hide in the day?'
… It is stiller than ever; the wind has fallen.
The moist air brings,
To mix with the spicy breath of the young break-wind macrocarpa,
Wafts of the acrid, familiar aroma of slowly-smouldering logs.
And hark, through the empty silence and dimness
Solemnly clear,
Comes the wistful, haunting cry of some lonely, far-away morepork,
'*Kia toa!* Be Brave!'

—Night is come.
Now the gully is hidden, the logs and the paddock all hidden.
Brightly the Stars shine out!…
The sky is a wide black paddock, without any fences,
The Stars are its shining logs;
Here, sparse and single, but yonder, as logg'd-up for burning,
Close in a cluster of light.
And the thin clouds, they are the hills,
They are the spurs of the heavens,
On whose steepnesses scatter'd, the Star-logs silently lie:
Dimm'd as it were by the distance, or maybe in mists of the mountain
Tangled—yet still they brighten, not darken, the thick-strewn slopes!
But see! these hills of the sky
They waver and move! their gullies are drifting, and driving;
Their ridges, uprooted,
Break, wander and flee, they escape! casting careless behind them
Their burdens of brightness, the Stars, that rooted remain.
—No! they do not remain. No! even they cannot be steadfast.
For the curv'd Three (that yonder
So glitter and sparkle
There, over the bails),
This morning, at dawn,
At the start of the milking,
Stood pale on the brink of yon rocky-ledged hill;
And the Cross, o'er the viaduct
Now, then was slanting,
Almost to vanishing, over the snow.
So, the Stars travel, also?
The poor earthly logs, in the wan earthly paddocks,
Never can move, they must stay;
But over the heavenly pastures, the bright, live logs of the heavens
Wander at will, looking down on our paddocks and logs, and pass on.
'O friendly and beautiful Live-Ones!
Coming to us for a little,

Then travelling and passing, while here with our logs we remain,
 What are you? Where do you come from?
 Who are you? Where do you go?'

Ah, little Questioner!
Son of the Burnt Bush;
Straightly pent 'twixt its logs and ridges,
To its narrow round of monotonous labours
Strictly tether'd and tied:
And here to-night, in the holiday twilight,
Conning, counting, and clasping as treasures,
Whatsoever about your unchanging existence
Moves and changes and lives:—
One delight have you miss'd, and that one of more import than any:
More quick than the River, more fraught than the Mail-Train,
More certain to move than the stars in their courses,
The most radiant wonder, the rarest excitement of all.
 *What is it? Oh, what can it be?*
 —It is you, little Thor! 'Tis yourself!
 Little, feeble, ignorant, destitute:—
 Wondering, questioning, conscious, alive!
A Mind that moves 'mid the motionless matter:
'Mid the logs, a developing Soul:
From the battle-field bones of a ruin'd epoch,
Life, the Unruin'd, freshly upspringing.
Life, Re-creator of life!

Yea, spark of Life!
Begotten, begetter of changes:
Yea, morn of Man,
Creature design'd to create:
Offspring of elements all, appointed their captain and ruler:
Here dawning, here sent
To this, thy disconsolate kingdom—
What change, O Changer! wilt thou devise and decree?

Hail to thy god-ship, O Thor! Good luck to the Arm with the
    Hammer!
Good luck to that little right arm!
Green Bush to the Moa, Burnt Bush to the resolute Settler!
In strenuous years ahead,
Wilt thou wield the axe of the Fire?
Wilt thou harness the horse of the Wind?
Shall not the Sun with his strong hands serve thee, and the tender
    hands of the Rain?
Daytime and Night spring in turn to thy battle,
Time and Decay run in yoke to thy plough,
And Earth, from the sleep of her sorrow
Waked at thy will, with an eager delight rise, requicken'd, and heartily
    help thee?
—Till the charr'd logs vanish away;
Till the wounds of the land are whole:
Till the skeleton valleys and hills
With greenness and growing, with multiplied being and movement,
Changeful, living, rejoice!

Yea, newly-come Soul!
Here on Earth, from what region unguess'd at?
Here, to this rough and raw prospect, these back-blocks of Being,
    assign'd—
Lean, cumber'd with ruin, lonely, bristling with hardship,
A birthright that fires have been through—
What change, O Changer! creature, Creator of Spirit!
In this, thy burden'd allotment, wilt thou command and create?
    Finite, yet infinite,
    Tool, yet Employer,
    Of Forces Almighty,
    Beyond thee, within,—
What fires, of the Spirit, what Storms, wilt thou summon?
What Dews shall avail thee, what Sunbeams? What seed wilt thou
    sow?

Ease unto weaklings: to thews and to sinews, Achievement!
What pasture, Settler and Sovereign, shall be grazed from the soil-
    sweetening ashes?
What home be warm in the wild?
Nay, outflowing Heart! thou highway forward and back:
Thought-trains of the Mind! commercing with far-away worlds:
What up-country traffic and freight shall travel forth into the world?
What help will ye summon and send?
Spirit, deep in the Dark! with the light of what over-head worlds
Wilt thou in the Dark make friends?
O pioneer Soul! against Ruin here hardily pitted,
What life wilt thou make of existence?
Life! what more Life wilt thou make?

Ah, little Thor!
Here in the night, face to face
With the Burnt Bush within and without thee,
Standing, small and alone:
Bright Promise on Poverty's threshold!
    What art thou? Where hast thou come from?
    How far, how far! wilt thou go?

## *Maui's Fish*

(*After the Maori Legend*)

Maui, the Fisher, would have gone fishing
In the canoe with the sons of his mother;
He had a thought in his head.
But these Brothers begrudged him.
'He is young and audacious,' they grumbled, 'and wilful;
We are not too sure of his birth and his breeding;
His cunning is great, and his tricks are perdition;
What law does he follow? What reverence is his?

He will trick us, perchance, he will wreck, peradventure may drown
    us—
He surely will scare us!' said they.
'Bide thou here,' said these clever and cautious old brothers of Maui;
And forth on the broad breast of Ocean
Push'd the canoe, and were off
To their old fishing-ground.

Maui the Fisher paced on the sea-beach,
Thinking… thinking…
Working the while at the fish-hook he held in his fingers:
A very old bone he was carving and fitting,
And paving its hollow with blue-and-green *paua*,
*Paua*, purple-and-blue in the sun as the shimmering water,
In the sea-water, bright as the sun.
'Can I sail in the sea-weed?' says Maui;
And a fine tuft of hair he set on it,
Thinking… thinking…
And twisted a stout line upon it—
And behold! there he ended his toil and his thinking together!
'Ha, ha, ha!' laughs Maui the Fisher,
And looks out to sea!

Late that night, when these Brothers, safe back from their fishing,
Wearied with toil, snug and rounded with supper,
Snored in the *whare*,
Maui, the youngest, still hungry on purpose,
Alert and attentive—*Hush!*
Crept from the side of them—*Hush!*
From the warm *whare* creeps out, to the darkness,
Out, to the cold, lonely beach:
Finds the canoe, and there, under the bottom-boards,
Ha! in he crawls, and lies close.
Huge is the night, and the loneliness gruesome and terrible,
Sharp howls the wind, the old Sea moans there over his shoulder—

As a widow, a mother, they wail, at a death, at a *tangi*;
And the darkness was dreadful all round, a deep darkness of death!
'Laugh, O my heart!' murmurs Maui,
And waits for the Dawn.

And at Dawn come his Brothers, intent on their old daily duty—
In their old fishing-ground to catch fish.
And they look to their tiller, they look to their paddles,
But, under those sound boards amidship, what need to examine?
(Aha!)
'Now, where is our Maui, our fisher of fishers, this morning?
Full belly, sound sleeper, is simply out-witted,' they chuckle;
Then out on the laughing blue Ocean
Push forth their canoe, and are off
To their old fishing-ground—
To their old fishing-ground, indeed?
Maui is with them! Oho!

Paddle and paddle, paddle and paddle…
They had gone a long way,
To the first place for casting the hooks they were nearly arrived,
When Maui no more can keep silence. *Ho, ho!* and *Ha, ha!*—
Up pops his head at their horrified feet!
An earthquake! As huts in an earthquake,
Hither and thither they topple and tumble and sprawl.
Were they startled, those wary old Brothers? They nearly upset the
    canoe!
Were they vext? They were far from the land!
Now this way and that, as a *weka*, that peers for provision,
With faces wrath-wrinkled as mud-holes are wrinkled in summer,
They twisted their eyes and their necks, staying still on their paddles,
And piteously ask'd of each other:
'O Friends! What shall we do?
If we go on, and he with us,' they said, 'he will surely upset us,
If we go back, it is far—and what fish for our supper?'

'Cast him out!' whispers one. 'If we do, by some craft he will catch
  us—

Remember the noosing of *Ra*,' they reply, 'Remember the Theft of
  the Fire

(Fire, like Maui, perturbing and mischievous: true, 'tis a relish to
  fish)—

Who is safe from him? What shall we do?'

So they toss back and forth in the unsteady hold of their purpose,

Like river-waves, reaching the sea, but the tide flooding in.

Well, now, Maui had pity upon them.

'Let me paddle,' says Maui, 'or steer!'

But Oh, no, no, no!

'If he paddle,' say they, 'we are dead! he will surely capsize us;

If he steer,—we are wreck'd on some rock;

If we go on, misadventures are bound to befall us;

Back—one is fallen already, since where are our fish?

And, drown'd—alas, he would drown us!'

So, like men out at sea without paddles, they toss in a torment.

Till Maui had pity upon them again, and he said,

'Lo, in your confusion but now, how the waves were splashed over!

Keep me—to bale the canoe.'

Then speechless they sat, looking one at the rest,

Till one hopefully said,

'Well, he cannot do much with a baler!'

So then, o'er the bright lips of Ocean, up-bursting with laughter,

These Brothers went cautiously steering and paddling,

While Maui (a shell was his baler)

Baled out the canoe.

Now, pay attention! Behold,

Every shellful he baled from the boat, lo it was but a shellful,

Till, throwing it over, he stretch'd it—no longer mere shellfuls,

Murmuring *karakias*, secretly chanting enchantments.

Seas! he threw overboard.

The water spread... spread..., the land faded, faded... and faded...
'Hold! Stop!' cried the Brothers. 'Where are we?
Far, far past our fishing-ground! Put back, and quickly!' they cry.
'Ah, not yet!' Maui pleads, 'O my Brothers, a little way further!
I know of a place where the fish are as fern in the forest,
So many! and fat as fat pigeons, and sweeter than berry-fed pigeons,
    those fish!
Let us on!' And his tongue was of oil, and his words as a feast in
    the cooking;
(He knew what they wished) and their ears and their hearts were
    bemused.
On, onward they went:
Paddle and paddle, paddle and paddle and paddle...
The Sun looking on from the North, and Maui still baling and baling.
Till once more spake the Brothers:
'No man hath fished here since the days of our fathers; here anchor!'
'Not yet, Ah, not yet!' Maui said; 'A canoe's length, a little way further!
Ah, Brothers, those fish! So immense
That one piece of one fish will most nobly provide for our supper,
So bold, they will race to the hook, and two castings will fill us,
The wink of an eye see us full.'
Aha! Bright was his bait, and he knew what he wanted,
By the ear and the stomach he caught them, these Brothers, these fish!

Paddle on, paddle on, paddle on...
Now the land is gone from their gaze;
To the edge of the world they are come!
Now the Sea was their world,
And the Sun from the opposite side look'd upon them,
He looked from the West, and their spirits grew dark,
Their hearts rolled in their breasts!
'Never man can have fished here before. Let us anchor!' they pleaded;
And Maui said, 'Anchor, and fish!'
For he knew where he was, and he knew he was where he would be.

Oh! Oh, those fish!… Enough! It was even as he said—
So many! so large! and they surely desired to get eaten!
Lo! at the cast of the hook, how they came flocking, and flocking!
Two castings apiece, and behold! the canoe, it was full!
Great then were the hearts of these Brothers! They said,
'It is well! and now let us for home.'
But Maui said humbly, 'O Brothers!
Here is one without fish. Behold, I have had neither share of the
    sport or the spoil.
Lend me a hook, O Brother!—Brother! lend me thy hook'
(To one and another he said it). But they taunted him, all, and refused.
'Fishers have hooks, not the maggot that hides in the timber.'
'Canst thou fish with a hook, little Trickster, indeed? but try fishing
    without!'
'Yet will I fish,' answers Maui, and lo! lo! the wonder.
They murmur, admiring, in envy they muse, and amazement,
As he draws from his mat the carv'd fish-hook,
The jaw-bone well carv'd of his heroine ancestress.
Bright in the sunlight the *paua* that lined it,
The hair that adorn'd it waved bright in the wind.
'Ha, ha, ha!' laughs Maui the Fisher,
The Sun and the Sea also laugh, when they look on that hook!
But—where was the bait?
'O my brothers,' says Maui, 'Behold
To what catch I encouraged you hither!
Can we verily take it all home? See the gunwale, how low in the water!
Spare me, spare me one morsel of all these great fish of your fishing
For bait to my hook.'
But they jeer'd in delight: 'Aha! So art thou caught, little *Pipi*?
O friend! what is the use of fine fish-hooks, and ever so fine,
Without bait?' And they gave him no bait.

So then Maui bethought him.
He smote on his nostril. The blood of his head ran out, copious and
    living—

With his blood he baited his hook.
And, now laughing no longer, but grave, and firm of attention,
He casts the hook into the Sea.
'Prosper it, O Tangaroa!'
And Tangaroa,
Lord of the deep and the surface,
Lurer to enterprise, lover of daring adventure,
Heard!
A bite! a bite!
Lift it! Pull! Pull!
Oh, the weight!
Hold, hook of noble extraction! Hold, trustworthy well-twisted line!
Tug! Pull, pull!
'A rock! 'Tis a rock thou hast cleverly caught,' cry the Brothers—
No! for in comes the line… in… in…
' 'Tis a whale. This great Maui! so mighty, no lesser fish suits him.
The water is troubled; I said if he came, so would grief.'
And truly the water was troubled, a wave struck the side,
The sun sank, it grew chilly and dark.
'The old ground was good. We were fools to have ventured beyond
    it—
Give up, Maui! Let us go home.'
His back is bent, his muscles are tauten'd,
Sweat pours in the Sea… Pull! Pull!
'A *taniwha*, surely! some terrible monster has caught us!
Give over!' He would not. Pull! Pull!
Then, 'Over with *him*!'—urges one, but the rest were afraid.
'Cut his line!' But they could not: it held.

And now the waves bubble and gurgle indeed!
A storm he is raising, this fish!
Splash! Now the water foams into the boat—Now the Brothers must
    bale her,
Maui the Fisher would fish.
… Oh, the swirl and the tumult! Oh, waves, like great ridges and
    gullies!

Like a bladder of kelp, rooted firm there below, like a kite of the waves,
The canoe jerks and staggers. Bale! Bale!
Bale!… All the fish must go out!
Ah, sweet food! Ah, the horrible tricks of this mischievous Maui!
Ah, the huge billows bursting… Bale! Bale!…
—Darkness, tumult and storm,
Thus all the night through, Maui fought with his fish.

Toward the Dawn,
Lo, a Sea of thick shining! Behold the thick waves of great fishes!
This way and that way darting and shooting in masses,
Anxious, in haste to escape.
What is lifting them? *Pull!*
What is under them? *Pull!*…
The first beam strikes on the water…
The Brothers rub at their eyes… *O pull!*
*Pull!* What is this that they see?

      Thro' the waves, flashing!
      To the light, flashing!
   Bright, bright up-bursting, startling the light.—
Oh, the sharp spears and spikes! Oh, the sparkle of summits of crystal,
       Spring up, up!
Tongariro! O Taranaki,
Your splendour! your shooting of spear-points, keen, sea-wet, to
   the sun!
Ruapehu, Kaikoura, Aorangi, Tara-rua, long-arm'd Ruahine!—
Midsummer clouds, curling luminous up from the sky-line:
Far-fallen islands of light, summon'd back to the sun:
Soaring *kahawai-birds*—
How ye soar'd, shining pinions! straight into the heaven high above
   you:
How ye shot up, bright Surprises! seizing, possessing the sky:
How firm, great white Clouds, ye took seat!

Pull, Maui! Pull!

For what follows, beneath them?

A waving, a waving and weaving of light and of darkness—

A waving of hands and of hair in the dance!

Lo, is it a garden of kelp?

Is it Night, coming up from the deep, up through fold upon fold of
   the Sea?

Pull!

Behold, it approaches! it darkens, it pierces the water—Lo! Lo!

Tree-tops! Lo, waving of branches! Lo, mosses and fern of the forest!

How sweet on the salt came the breath of the forest, that summer
   sea-morning!

Sweet on the spacious silence the ring of the Tui's rich throat!

*Kauri* and *Totara*, *Rimu*, and *Matai* and *Maire*,

Red-as-blood *Rata*, and bright-as-blood *Pohutu-kawa*,

*Manuka* dark-eyed, Convolvulus, Clematis star-eyed—

The glittering of you that morning! fresh, dripping with dews of
   the Ocean,

New rays to the young, early sun!

The host of your *taua*, address'd as to fight! of your lances and *meres*
   of green-stone,

Bristling all suddenly upward, lustrously tossing in glory,

A green sea, high in the air!

Pull on! Pull away!

I see shining and shining below here.

Is there a Sun in the Sea? a young Sky in the water?

A Sea, deep in Sea?

Or is a great paua-shell, empty, vividly variegated,

Shadow playing with shine, blue and green in the arms of each other,

As they lie on the lap of the Sea?

Lo! it nears! it arrives! on the face of the water it floats—

Land—Ho! Land!

Yea, sparkling with freshness, audacious with newness, laughing
   with light,

Land! a young Land from the Sea!
A dark land, of forest; a bright land, of sky and of summits,
Of tussock sun-gilded, of headlands proclaiming the sun:
Tattoo'd with blue—behold Waikato! lo Wanganui!
Ey'd with quick eyes—Wakatipu, and over there Taupo:
Plumed with sky-feathers, with clouds and with snow: begirt with
    the mat of the Ocean
Border'd with foam, with fine fringes of sand, with breast-jewels of
    clear-coloured pebbles:—
Up it sprang, out it burst from the folds of the foam, out it stood,
Bare-bright on the jewel-bright Sea:—
A new Land!

There it stood!
And the Sea, now at rest, laid her down with her arms round about it,
Thrusting the tongue and the touches of love 'gainst the limbs of
    the living,
Caressing her newly-born, laughing and singing for joy.
And, up-coiling his line, disentangling his fish-hook, now Maui
    laugh'd also—
'Ha, ha, ha!' laughed Maui the Fisher,
'Behold, I have caught me a Fish!'
Enough—Even so!
With a hook of the Dead, with a bait of the Living,
With the thought of his head, with the blood of his body, the sweat
    of his heart,
With pangs and with laughter, with labour and loss,
He truly had caught him a fish—the canoe was aground—
O *Te Ika a Maui*—The Fish!

But turn now your eyes on those worthy, wise Brothers of Maui,—
With grimaces nibbling their faces, with eyes and with mouths round
    as sea-eggs,
They squat on their haunches, stuck still:
Dumb as heads in the old days held fast in the mouth of the oven,

Dumb as fish,—who would ever have thought it?
But hear now their guile!

'O my Brothers,' said Maui,
'Meet is it I go with thank-offerings to thank Tangaroa—
Tangaroa, who gave me this fish:
Rangi also, and Tawhiri-matea, who hid it below.
But abide till I come!' he besought them with earnest persuasions,
'Till these gods are bespoken, with hand or with foot,
O defile not my fish!
When I come, I will portion it all.' So he went.
But what then said these Brothers?
Aha! As the *kotare*, perched and asleep, hears the fish-rippled water, and straightway awakes,
They awoke!
'Who is Maui?' said they 'who that babe, with his portion, and portion?
What wits he of division? What recks he of custom, time-honour'd?
What does a young man know?
*His* fish! Was it not *our* canoe?
Come!' They trampled his words underfoot, and leapt out on the beaches.
'This my land!' shouted one, and he set up his paddle upon it,
'This to me!' 'This to me!' cried they all;
They wrangled and strove.
But the land, this *Te Ika a Maui*,
Beholding their impudence, seeing their greed and their quarrel,
Laugh'd—for they were not her master—
Laugh'd! Lo, she wrinkled her skin, shook her sides, laugh'd wide with her lips...
'Ha, ha!' and 'Ha, ha!'...
Till Maui, returning, instead of a smooth land, and Brothers in waiting,
Found this fellow, sprawl'd on the top of a sudden-reared mountain:
That, deep in a gully new-cloven: this other, head-first in a swamp;

And all abash'd and ashamed.
Louder then laugh'd Maui the Fisher.
'Ha, ha! Well done, the land!
Ha, Tangaroa, well done!
My Fish, my Fish, is alive!'

This is the tale of the Fishing of Maui,
Of the birth of New Zealand, *Te Ika a Maui.*
Hear yet!
I speak but one little word more.

Still alive is that Fish!
Here, on the edge of the world, on the rim of the morning,
She stands, Tangaroa's dear daughter, a vigorous virgin,
Fresh from the foam.
Still the daylight is young in her eyelids, and on her full forehead;
Her brown limbs gleam from the bath,
Dew is yet in her wind-tossing hair.
The wild winds are her walls, and she stands here, untamed as
     sea-water,
Brave with the heart of the Ocean, sweet with the heart of the Sun.
Ay!
A sea-wind for freshness, a sea-wave for brightness,
A sea-sunrise for beauty, a strong sea for strength,
Here she stands, Maui's Fish, here she shines, a new Land from the
     Ocean,
Alive 'mid the ever-live Sea.

Alive! Yea, Te Ika—
Of the Bone of the Past, of the Blood of the Present,
Here, at the end of the earth, in the first of the Future,
Thou standest, courageous and youthful, a country to come!
Lo, thou art not defiled with the dust of the Dead, nor beclouded
     with thick clouds of Custom:
But, springs and quick sources of life all about thee, within thee,
Splendid with freshness, radiant with vigour, conspicuous with hope,

Like a beacon thou beckonest back o'er the waters, away o'er the world:
The while, looking ahead with clear eyes,
Like Maui, thou laugh'st, full of life!

And do not regard overmuch
Those tedious old Brothers, that still must be pribbling and prab-
bling about thee
(Paddlers inshore: when a Maui has fish'd, then they claim the
canoe!)…
Laugh at them, Land!
They are old: are they therefore so wise?
Thou art young, Te Ika: be young!
Thou art new: be thou new!
With keen sight, with fresh forces, appraise those old grounds of
their vaunting,
Dip in deep dew of thy seas what swims yet of their catch, and renew
it,—
The rest, fish very long caught,
Toss it to them!
And address thee to catches to come.
Rich hauls to bold fishers, new sights to new sight, a new world to
new eyes,
To discoverers, discoveries! Yea,
Offspring of Maui! recall the experience of Maui
A dead fish he did not receive it? No, No!
He endured, he adventured, he went forth, he experimented,
He found and he fetch'd it, alive!

Yea, alive! a Fish to give thanks for.
Ah, ah, Tangaroa, well done!
Thou livest, Te Ika a Maui!
Enough! My last word:—
Live! Dare! Be alive!

## from *The Paddock*

We were young—too young, I said,
When he first proposed the plan;
Mother blind, my hands were full;
We could wait awhile to wed?
Andrew smiled, and shook his head,
Took the section, and began,
Working on the road awhile,
As he could, to fall and burn.
—Eh! we had a lot to learn.
We were young and hopeful-hearted.
Ten years we've been married now—
But it's twenty since we started.

First, there came his accident:
Weeks of Hospital: next year,
Debt, instead of Bush, to clear!
Then, wet seasons, and he had
No help, and the 'burns' were bad.
Next, his father died, and Don
Was but quite a laddie, so
Andrew took their farming on,
And his own just had to go.
Then, at length, when years had seen
Mostly all the young ones wed:
When the land was coming clean,
Fences up, and shearing-shed,
Apple-trees in bearing round
Such a well-stock'd garden-ground,
And the homestead all but done,
And the battle all but won:—
Came the big Bush-fire! So then
All was to begin again.

Well, again it *was* begun.
What you paddocks lack'd in luck
Was made up to you in pluck,
Oh, it was! and patient skill,
Yes, and splendid, stubborn will.

'Twasn't long from that, when first
Mother, and then Father, died.
All the rest were off and settled,
Janet, just, was left beside.
Then: 'I'm warning you; think well!'
Andrew said, 'I'm still behind,
But—O lassie! should you mind?
Could you manage? 'Twill be tough…
Could you live in half a home?'
'Yes!' I told him—if 'twas his,
'Half of half would be enough';
And he answer'd, 'Thank God! Come!'

Aunt took Janet for a while,
And I came,—came here! The track
Lost itself in rocks and bogs,
And through grass less green than black
With the pell-mell stumps and logs.
Suddenly it stopp'd—I saw,
Thro' the whips of driving rain,
And a blasted *Rimu*'s boughs,
—Oh! so naked, rough and raw,
Stumps and logs behind, before,
Paddock to the very door—
Just a clearing, and a house.
Some potatoes round it grew,
Here and there, a sapling tree
Was just big enough to see,
That was all, and that was—You!

Inside, Oh! 'twas worse. I mind,
Shelves and doors were all to find,
Only two rooms even lined,
And the stove dump'd down outside.
I was tired—I could have cried!
Andrew stood and look'd at it,
Then he turn'd, and look'd at me
Struggling that he shouldn't see.
'Ay!' says he, 'So little done!'
Oh, that dear, good, grieving face,
And that disappointed tone,
Fire and wine they were within me!—
'No!' I cried, 'So much *begun*!
Why it's just a new-made world
Given to us two to run—
*Us*, lad! Won't that mend the moan?
Us! not you, nor me alone.'

    \*   \*   \*   \*

              Wash up the dishes,
Sweep out the kitchen, put on dinner (Oh,
That hateful, daily, never-done-with dinner!
Why do we have to eat?), then, that disposed of—
Oh, what's there ever to look forward to?
Well, it is coach-day, though; I can ride Dapple
Out to the road, and take these strawberries down,
And wait for mail—and, save newspapers, get none!
Oh dear! There's scarcely anyone goes by coach,
There's never anyone up or down the road,
Much less along the track, of course. Heigh-ho!
Eternal Paddock's *dull*!… Then, when I'm back…
Oh, what does it matter? Play with Andy, read
Some stale old book, I've read six hundred times,
Get tea, and clear it; then—the empty evening!
Once in a blue moon, some one may drop in—
Night after night, they don't, and there I'll sit,

Jean's frock, or Andy's overall to patch,
While Andrew reads aloud, of wheat and wool,
And 'Lizebeth listens. Nine o'clock at last!
I'll light my candle, let out, full, the yawn
Kept in since daybreak, get to bed.—That's all!
That's my whole day.

                To-morrow? Same old sorrow!
Cook, clean—the same tame humdrum… I forgot—
Churning's thrown in—it's Friday. Every Friday
These last four years… (Let's see, I'd just left school
When 'Lisbeth sent for me… I'm eighteen now—
Yes! four whole years, except that trip to Aunt's)
I've churned! I've washed on every possible house—
Iron'd each Tuesday, Wednesdays, clean'd the house,—
Oh! haven't I done enough? And, when it's done,
What does it all amount to? where's it gone?
That is the worst of all! If one had slaved
Straight on at anything that monstrous time,
I guess there would be something, at the end,
*Done*, and to show for it. But just look at me!
Four years… say seven-and-forty solid months,
Over a thousand days!… I've faithfully
Roasted and fried, made beds and bread-and-butter,
Scrubb'd, rubb'd, and all the rest—with what result?
What's in the house this moment? Tumbled beds,
An empty larder, and a foot-mark'd floor!
That's all. With all the doing, nothing's Done;
With all the endless making, nothing's Made;
There's nothing come of all the eternal drudge,
Except—the need to drudge all over again!
Oh, who'd be a housekeeper? week in, week out,
The same old stupid treadmill; kick your heels,
Beat time, but never get on. I'm sick of it!
What will the next three years be like, I wonder?
Different, if I can manage it,—that I know!

# PART II

*Brown Bread from a Colonial Oven*

# Pipi on the Prowl

Pipi was very happy. To an indifferent observer, it is true, the little mummy-like old Maori woman, bundled about with a curious muddle of rag-bag jackets and petticoats, and hobbling along the high-road on crippled bare brown feet, might have presented a spectacle more forlorn than otherwise. But then, what does the indifferent observer ever really see? That grotesque and pitiful exterior was nothing but an exterior; and it covered an escaping captive thing: it clothed incarnate Mirth. For Miria had gone to town, and Pipi, one whole long afternoon, was free!

She chuckled as she thought of Miria—Miria the decorous, Miria the *pakeha* coachman's wife, Miria, who wore tan shoes. Miria did not like her grandmother to go roaming at her own sweet will along the roads; she did not even like her to smoke; what she did like was to have her squatted safe at the *whare* door, holding on to little Hana, whose kicking really began to be painful, and looking out that little Himi did not get hold of the axe and chop himself to bits. She had left her like that half an hour ago; probably she imagined her to be still like that—submissive, stationed, and oh, how lacklustre, how dull! Well, Pipi might perhaps be a little *porangi* (crazy) at times, but she was never anything like so *porangi* as that. How lucky that Ropata's wife was a trustworthy crony! How fortunate that the babies could neither of them speak! Pipi smiled, and showed her perfect teeth; she took out, from deep recesses of her raiment, her treasured pipe, and stuck it in her mouth. *E! Ka pai te paipa!*—a good thing, the pipe! There was no *topeka* (tobacco) in it, to be sure; but who could say whence *topeka* might not come, this golden afternoon? To those newly at liberty all the world belongs. And, like stolen waters, stolen sport is sweet. No urchin who, having safely conveyed himself away at last out of earshot of mother or teacher, bounds breathless to the beloved creek where 'bullies' wait the hook, knows more of the mingled raptures of lawlessness and expectation than this old great-grandmother Pipi did, out upon the high-road, out upon the hunt!

Although it was midwinter, the afternoon was warm—there is never really cold weather upon that sheltered northern coast. The road ran right round the head of the league-long harbour, and showed a splendid view; for the tide was in; every cove and inlet was full, and the sinuous, satin-blue sheen of the water reflected with the utmost fidelity every one of the little long, low spits, emerald-turfed and darkly crowned with trees, that fringed, as with a succession of piers, the left-hand shore; while the low, orange-coloured cliffs of the fern-flats opposite burned in the brilliant sun like buttresses of gold. But what was a view to Pipi? Her rheumy old brown eyes sought but the one spot, where, far down the glittering water-way, and close to the short, straight sapphire line that parted the purple Heads and meant the open sea, the glass of the township windows sent sparkles to the sun. The township—seven miles away, and Miria not there yet! *Ka pai!* Pipi was ready for whatever fish Tangaroa might kindly send her on dry land, but meanwhile freedom, simple freedom, mere lack of supervision, was in itself enough; and happily, happily she trudged along, nodding, smiling, and sucking vigorously at her empty pipe.

Before very long she came to the river—the sinister-looking river, black and sluggish, that drains the valley-head. In the swamp on the other side of the long white bridge, dark *manuka*-bushes with crooked stems and shaggy boles, like a company of uncanny crones under a spell, stood knee-deep in thick ooze; some withered *raupo* desolately lined the bank above. Even on that bright day, this was a dismal place, and the *raupo*, with its spindly shanks and discoloured leaves fluttering about them, looked lamentably like poor Pipi. *Poor* Pipi, indeed? Dismal place? Huh! what does a fool know?

With brightened eyes, with uncouth gestures of delighted haste, out across the bridge scurried Pipi, slithered down into the swamp, clutched with eager claws at a muddy lump upon the margin, and emitted a deep low grunt of joy. Old snags, quite black with decay, lay rotting round her, and the stagnant water gave forth a most unpleasant smell. But what is foulness when glory beckons through it? Squatting in the slime, her tags and trails of raiment dabbling in and out of the black water, Pipi washed and scraped, scraped and washed, and finally lifted up and out into the sunshine with a grin of delight, a great golden pumpkin, richly streaked with green. The glint of its rind had caught her eye from the other side of the bridge. Evidently it had fallen from some passing cart, and rolled down into the swamp. It was big; it was heavy; it was sound. The goodness of this pumpkin! the triumph of this find! Pipi untied one of her most extra garments, tied the treasure securely in it, slung the bundle on her back as though it had been a baby, and went on.

From the river, the road runs straight uphill, through a cutting betwen high banks of fern and gorse, with a crumbly crest of *papa* clay boldly yellow on the full blue sky. The road is of yellow *papa* also, and unmetalled, and rather heavy. Pipi grunted a good deal as she toiled up it; and about halfway up stood still to get her breath, for the pumpkin, precious as it was, lay like lead upon her frail old shoulders. Why! at the very top of the bank, glaring in the sunshine against the yellow *papa*, what was that? A white paper only, with nothing in it—or a white paper parcel? Steep as the bank was, go she must, of course, and see; and up, pumpkin and all, she climbed. Aha! Something inside. What?… Bread; and, inside the bread? Jam; thick, sweet, deep-red jam, very thick, very sweet, *very* good!

Next to tobacco, Pipi loved sweet things. She did not expend much pity upon the school-child that, heedlessly running along the top edge of the bank that morning, had lost its lunch and spent a hungry dinner-hour; neither did the somewhat travelled appearance of the sandwich trouble her. She scrambled down again on to the firmer footing of the road, and there she stood, and licked and licked at the jam. Miria's face, if she had caught her at it! Oho, that face!—the very fancy of its sourness made the tit-bit sweeter. The bread itself she threw away. Her stomach was not hungry, Miria saw to that; but her imagination was, and that was why this chance-come, wayside dainty had a relish that no good, dull dinner in the *whare* ever had. Sport was good to-day. First that pumpkin, now this jam! *Ka pai* the catch! What next?

She resumed her journey up-hill, but had no sooner reached the top than she suddenly squatted down on the bank by the roadside, as if at a word of command, with next to no breath left in her lungs, but hope once more lively in her heart—for here, surely, advancing to meet her, was the Next—a tall young *pakeha* woman, with a basket on her arm. Only a woman. That was a pity, for there was the less chance of *topeka*; still, what had that kit got in it?

Pipi knew all about strategical advantages by instinct. She sat still and waited on her hill-top as her forefathers had sat still on theirs, and waited for the prey. Soon it came; a little breathless, and with footsteps slackening naturally as they neared the brow, just as Pipi had foreseen. Yes, she would do, this *pakeha*, this pigeon; she would pay to be plucked. She was nicely dark and stout; she smiled to herself as she walked; and such good clothes upon the back denoted certainly a comfortable supply of *hikapeni* (sixpences) in the pocket.

'*Tenakoe! Tenakoe!*' (greeting!) cried Pipi, skipping up from her bank with a splendid assumption of agility, as the stranger came alongside; and extending her hand, expanding her smile, and wagging her wily old head, as if this strange young *pakeha* were her very dearest friend in all the world. And the bait took! The *pakeha*, too, stretched forth her hand, she, also, smiled. A catch, a catch to Pipi the fisher! Let us, though, find out first how much she knows, this fish... Not to speak the Maori tongue means not to read the Maori mind, so:

'*E hoa!*' says Pipi leisurely, '*E haere ana koe i whaea?*'

Good! it is all right. The *pakeha* stands still, laughs, and says, 'Oh, please say it in English!'

She is ignorant, she is affable, she is not in a hurry. She will do, this nice young *pakeha*! Pipi translates.

'Where you goin'?'

'I am going—oh, just along this road for a bit,' says the girl vaguely.

Pipi considers. 'Along the road,' in the stranger's present direction, means back towards home for Pipi; it would surely be a pity to turn back so soon? A fish on the line, however, is worth two in the water; also, after the feast is eaten, cannot the empty basket be thrown away? in other words, as soon as ever it suits her, cannot she pretend to be tired and let the stranger go on alone? Of course she can! So Pipi says, 'Me, too,' and, turning her back, for the time being, upon the enticement of the open road ahead, goes shambling back, hoppity-hop, down the hill again, at the side of her prey. She shambles slowly, too, by way of a further test, and, see, the girl instinctively adapts her pace. Excellent! Oh, the pleasantness, the complaisance, of this interesting young friend! Pipi takes hold of her sleeve, and strokes it.

'Ah, the good coat,' she cries, with an admiration that she does not need to assume. 'He keep you warm, my word! My coat, see how thin!' and she holds out for inspection a corner of her topmost covering, an old blouse of faded pinkish print, phenomenally spotted with purple roses. It is true that she has the misfortune to hold out also, quite by mistake, a little bit of the layer next beneath, which happens to be a thick tweed coat; but this she drops immediately, without an instant's delay, and it is well known that *pakehas* have as a rule only pebbles in their eye-sockets—they see nothing; while their ears, on the other hand, are as *kokota*-shells, to hold whatever you please to put in. 'I cold, plenty, plenty,' says Pipi accordingly, with a very well-feigned shiver. 'How much he cost, your good, warm coat?'

'Why, I don't quite know,' replies the pakeha. 'You see, it was a present; somebody gave it me.'

'Ah, nobody give poor Pipi,' sighs Pipi, very naughtily. Is it a good thing or not, that two of the Colonel's old flannel shirts, Mrs Cameron's knitted petticoat, and Miria's thickest dress, all of them upon her person at that moment, have no tongues. 'Nobody give *kai* (food) even. What you got in your big kit?' she asks coaxingly. '*Plenty* big kit!'

'Ah, nothing at all. Only air. It's just cramful of emptiness,' says the girl, sadly shaking her head. 'What you got on your back in the bundle there? Plenty big bundle!'

It is useless, of course, to deny the existence of so plain a fact as that pumpkin. Why had not Pipi had the wit to hide it in the fern?

'On'y punkin,' she says, with a singular grimace, expressive at first of the contemptibility of all the pumpkin tribe, then changing instantly to a radiant recognition of their priceless worth, for her mind has been

'Stung with the splendour of a sudden thought.'

'He *fine* punkin, big, *big* punkin,' she cries, and then, munificently, 'You give me coat, I give you this big, big punkin!' She exhibits her treasure as one astounded at her own generosity.

The *pakeha*, however, seems astounded at it, too.

'Why!' says she, 'my coat is worth at least three thousand pumpkins.'

Perhaps it is? Pipi tries to imagine three thousand pumpkins lying spread before her, with a view to assessing their value; but, not unnaturally, fails. Ah well! Bold bargaining is one weapon, but tactful yielding is another.

'*E!* You give me *hikapeni*, then, I give you punkin.' She concedes, with an air of reckless kindness, and a hope of sixpence-worth of *topeka* to be purchased presently on the sly from Wirimu, the gardener.

But 'I don't care much for pumpkins,' says the stupid *pakeha*. 'And I haven't any *hikapeni*,' she adds. The stingy thing! A fish? why, the creature is nothing at all but an empty cockle-shell not worth the digging. And Pipi is just thinking that she shall soon feel too tired to walk a single step farther, when, suddenly producing a small, sweetly-familiar-looking packet from her coat, 'You like cigarettes?' inquires the *pakeha*.

'*Ai! Homai te hikarete! Ka pai te hikarete!* (Yes! Give me a cigarette! I do like cigarettes),' cries Pipi, enraptured, and the *pakeha* holds out the packet. Alas! there are only two cigarettes left in it, and manners will permit of Pipi's taking only one. This is very trying.

'You smoke?' she asks innocently. The girl denies it, of course, as Pipi knew she would: these *pakeha* women always do, and Miria, their slavish advocate and copyist, declares they speak the truth. Vain words; for, in the hotel at Rotorua, has not Pipi seen the very best attired of them at it? Moreover, why should this girl trouble to carry cigarettes if she does not smoke, herself? Plenty stupid, these *pakeha* women! Plenty good, however, their cigarettes, and greed (oh Miria!) overcoming manners, '*E!* You not smoke; you give me other *hikaret*', then,' she says boldly.

This miserable *pakeha*, however, proves to be as a pig, that, full of feed, yet stands with both feet in the trough—she only shakes her head, laughs sillily, and mutters some foolish remark about keeping the other for somebody else she might meet. Ah, well, never mind; Pipi has at least the one, and she would like to smoke it at once and make sure of it, but 'No right!' she says plaintively—she means 'no light'; she has no matches, and no more, it appears, has the *pakeha*. Boiled-headed slave! How, without matches, can she expect anybody to smoke her cigarettes?

'Perhaps this man has some,' suggests the *pakeha*, pointing to the solitary driver of a wagon coming down the hill behind them. She explains the predicament, and the man, with a good-natured smile, pours out half a boxful into Pipi's upstretched palms, and drives on. Ah, and perhaps he had *topeka* with him, too, real, good, dark, strong topeka in a stick; and, had Pipi only been wise enough to wait for him, and let this miserable person go by, she might by now, perhaps, have been having a real smoke. As for this *hikarete*, by the smell of it, Hana, aged thirteen months, could smoke it with impunity. No coat, no *kai*, no *hikapeni*, one *hikarete* of hay—Huh! the unprofitableness of this *pakeha*!

'You go on!' says Pipi, with an authoritative gesture. They have got as far as the bridge, and she squats down by her swamp. All that long hill to toil up again, too!

But behold, the black-hearted one at her side says, actually, 'Oh, I'm in no particular hurry. I think I'll sit down a bit, too,' and does so. Now, who that has found the *riwai* (potato) rotten wants to look at the rind?

Worse and worse—who can grow melons in mid-air, drink water without a mouth, or strike a match without something to strike it on?… What now? Here is the *pakeha*, in reply to this reproach, sticking out her thick leather boot right into Pipi's hand—an insult? She would kick the *hikaret'* out of it? Not so, for her eyes are soft… Swift as a weather-cock, round whirl Pipi's mobile wits.

'*E hoa!*' she cries with glee. 'You give me the *hu* (shoe)? Poor Pipi no *hu*, see! I think *ka pai*, you give me the hu.'

But the *pakeha* only shakes her head vigorously and laughs out loud. Is she *porangi* quite? No, not quite, it seems, for, taking a match from Pipi's hand, she strikes it on the clumsy sole, and lo! a flame bursts out. Pipi can light her *hikaret'* now, and does so, coolly using the pakeha's skirt the while, as a breakwind, for she may as well get out of her all the little good she can. And now, how to get rid of this disappointment, this addled egg, this little, little cockle with the big thick shell? Aha, Pipi knows. She will do what she has done so often with the prying Mrs Colonel Cameron— she will suddenly forget all her English, and hear and speak nothing but Maori any more. That will soon scrape off this *piri-piri* (burr). What shall she start by saying? Anything will do; and accordingly she mechanically asks again in Maori her first question, the question she asks every one, 'You are going, where?' But, O calamity! This time, the *pakeha*, the ignorant one, not only understands, but answers—and in the same tongue—and to alarming purpose!

'*E haere ana ahau ki a Huria* (I am going to Judaea),' she says. And Judaea is the name of Pipi's own *kainga*!

'*Ki a Huria!* and you know to speak the Maori!' she exclaims, startled into consternation.

'Only a very little as yet,' replies the girl. 'But Miria is teaching me.'

'Miria! which Miria?' cries Pipi, in an agony of foreboding.

'Why, Miria Piripi, Colonel Cameron's coachman's wife—*your* Miria, isn't she?' says this monster, with a sudden smile. 'She has told me about you, often.'

The truant who should suddenly see his captured 'bully' pull the hook out of its jaws in order to plunge it in his own, might very well feel as Pipi felt at this frightful moment. True enough, she had often heard Miria speak of the *pakeha* lady who came to visit Mrs Cameron and was 'always so interested in the natives'; and with the greatest care she had always kept out of her way, for Pipi had her pride—she resented being made into a show. And now—!

'Yes, and I have often seen you, too, though you may not have seen me,' pursued the relentless *pakeha*. 'You, and little Hana and Himi. Where are Hana and Himi now? I shall be sure to tell Miria I've met you,' she finished brightly.

Alas, alas for Pipi's sport! The fish had caught the fisher, and with a vengeance. She collected her scattering wits, and met the *pakeha*'s eye with a stony stare, for she came of a princely race; but cold, too, as a stone, lay the heart within her breast.

The heart of the *pakeha*, however, had also its peculiarities. For all she was a *pakeha*, clad in a fine coat, wearing boots, and carrying cigarettes about with her only by way of Maori mouth-openers: for all this, her heart was the heart of a fellow-vagabond. It understood. She *had* heard Miria, and Mrs Cameron too, talk of Pipi; but with a result of which those superior speakers were not conscious. How often she had silently sympathised with the poor old free-lance kept so straitly to the beaten track of respectability; how often she had wished for a peep at Pipi *au naturel*! And now she had got it; and she meant to get it again. She could not help a little mischievous enjoyment of the confusion so heroically concealed, but she took quick steps to relieve it.

'Well, I must go on,' she said briskly, rising as she spoke. 'Take the other cigarette, Pipi, and here's a shilling for some *topeka*. *E noho koe* (goodbye)! Oh, and, Pipi, don't let's tell Miria yet that we've met, shall we? It will be so nice for her to introduce us properly some day, you know!'

Pipi was game. '*Haere ra*' (good-bye) was all she answered, unemotionally. But she could not help one gleam of joy shooting out of her deep old eyes, and Lucy Willett saw it, and went on with a kindly laughter in her own.

That night, when she had rolled herself up in her blanket, and lain down on the *whare* floor (she disdained the foppishness of beds), Pipi glowed all through with satisfaction. Miria, on coming home, had found her seated, patient, pipeless, before the fire, Hana and Himi one upon each knee, both intact, both peacefully asleep; and had been so pleased with this model picture, as well as with the size of Pipi's pumpkin, that she had indulged her grandmother with schnapper for supper. And Pipi had found that pumpkin; she had harvested red jam from a fern-bank; she had had one cigarette to smoke, and with another had been able to encourage Ropata's wife to future friendly offices. More than that, she had had time for one blessed pipeful of real Derby, richly odorous, and in her most intimate garment of all could feel now, as she lay, safely knotted up, the rest of a whole stick. Nor was even that all. By some extraordinary good management that she herself did not quite understand, she had eluded the hook as it dangled at her very lips while yet she had secured the bait; and she had an instinctive, shrewd suspicion that, in cleverly causing the eye of the *pakeha* to wink at guilt, she had made sure of more patronage in the future. Who could tell? Perhaps, some fine day, that good thick coat, even, might find its way to Pipi's back. *Taihoa* (just wait)! Meanwhile, what a good day's sport!

# Grandmother Speaks

'And so you've pretty nearly all got telephones now, down in the Bay, an' can hear folks talk in Town? Well, well! An' Doubleday's buildin' another side on to his store—is he, now? little Johnny Doubleday, with his pants made out of a sack, that used to come a-tormentin' me for to give him a bite o' cold porridge, or a spud, in the days when provisions was run short, an' the whaleboats weather-stayed… *Johnny*, eh? Times change, so they do! What's that about the wharf? A new one already? Nonsense, girl! What, further out, you say, so bigger boats can come? Well, my word! I call that clear extravagance. Why, in them days all the wharf we had was the men's shoulders, an' they waist-deep in the sea…

'You like to hear tell o' them days? Do you, now? Well, an' I'm sure I like to talk of 'em. Get the kettle, an' put it on to boil, against your mother comes back; an' lay the tea-things too—then we can talk uninterrupted… Them days, eh! when the country an' me was young together, nigh on sixty years agone. Eh, dear me, them days! Only to think of 'em's like goin' out into the paddock right early when the sunshine's on the dew… Got the table all fixed? That's right. Then now we can begin.

'Well, father an' mother an' me come out together, as you know, early in the fifties, when I was but seven year old; an' nearly five months we was in comin', by the way; like everythin' else, ships was slower then. Soon almost as we'd a-landed here in port (that was pretty nigh nothin' else then, only tents, mind you), father, he got word for to go down to sawpit work, down along the coast. An' so, down along the coast we went, in a little bit of a cutter; an' all day long it took us, the men sayin' it was a good trip, too; an' by the time we got there, in the evenin', it was a-rainin', an' a-blowin' very cold;

an' never will I forget the look upon my poor dear mother's face as she sat in that boat a-gazin' an' a-gazin' on the land, an' a-seein' what she'd left London town for!

'It was just a little bit of a beach, at the top of a long narrow bay, that looked for all the world like a finger o' water, two or three miles long, stuck up in between the hills, an' a-dintin' of 'em down—but there! *you* know the Bay. It looked a bit different though in them days; for the hills, that's grass all over now, an' cocksfoot, was covered then with standin' Bush—there was Bush, and nothin' *but* Bush, for what looked like miles above the sand, as well as miles on either side of it; an' the only other thing to be glimpsed, strain your sight how you would, was three or four funny-lookin' huts, thatched with tussock-grass, an' a-standin' nigh on to the water's edge.

' "Cowsheds, I see," says mother, as they carried us out o' the boat, "but where do the poor things feed?" Poor mother! when they told her all the cows there was in Rakau could go through her weddin'-ring, an' the furthest house was ours, she just up an' dropped herself down upon a lump o' wet seaweed, an' burst out a-cryin'.

'It *was* hard on mother, mind you! In them days it was just about as bad as dyin', in one way, to come out to the Colonies. For you left all your friends behind you, an' you knew you could never get back no more for to see em'; leastways, people like mother couldn't. That was why it was best all to come in a family, when you could, fathers an' mothers, an' brothers an' sisters, an' the little children—all together, an' all a-lookin' the same way. But mother, there she'd left her own dear mother behind her, an' she'd been livin' in a nice three-storied house down Bermondsey way, with butcher and baker just round the corner, an' chimney-sweeps, an' newsboys an' all, up an' down the street—haven't she 'minded me about it, often and often? An' now here she was, come out to live in a one-roomed hut at this God-forsaken last end o' nowhere, right the other side the world; an' no way out o' the mess but to go straight through with it. Yes, there she sat an' cried, nor I don't wonder at it—no more I don't; an' couldn't be got even to look towards our hut, much less to go into it, whatever poor father could do; an' I sat there with her, while they got the chests and things out of the boat, an' cried too, for company, at first; only presently there was a two-three children come a-runnin' out o' one o' the other huts, an' them an' me stood a-lookin' at each other.

'An' then, all of a sudden, I give a great start, an' catched hold, *hard*, o' mother's hand; for there, stole up so silent out o' the trees that we hadn't heard him come, an' a-standin' straight up before us, was a great tall Maori man! Mother she looked up, saw him, give one screech that you'd think they could a-heard in Town, an' was off into that there hut of ours, an' me with her, an' the door shut, with both our backs against it, before you could ha' blinked. In them days, you see, a blanket was a native's full dress, an' they mostly didn't trouble to dress full, an' that man hadn't.

'Well, but you can get used to pretty much anything, bless you! an' specially when you must. It wasn't very long before the Bay was home to me, an' every day a holiday. Not that I hadn't work to do—every one in them days had to do their bit, soon as they was born, almost; but there wasn't any school (another thing to tease poor mother, but I know it never did me, not till I was grown up), an' all you did was done out in the open, an' there was the sea, an' the Bush, an' I'd my little mates in the other *whares*; an' then, everythin', pretty near, was contrivance—an' young ones always like that; it's as good as a game. We'd no oven, I remember, nor no camp-oven neither, at the start; Mother used to bake in her biggest saucepan. An' we'd no bedsteads; father, he boarded over the floor, first thing, an' mother used to keep it strewn deep with fresh sawdust from the pits (bright reddish-brown it was to look at, an' as *sweet*! for nearly all the trees was pine), and she'd a-brought out her feather-beds with her, an' we spread 'em on the floor an' slept soft. For all chairs an' table, we'd our wooden chests that we brought with us; an' mother, I remember, made curtains of a bit o' print she had, because she couldn't abide the sight of a naked window—it looked so mean, she said. Mother, she got more contented, after a bit, specially after your great-uncle Mat was born; but she never come to like the life as father an' me did. See England again? Poor soul, poor soul, nay, that she never did!

'What did we do all day, an' how did we live? I'll tell you. The men (they was all sorts, from them that lived respectable in the huts alongside ours with their wives an' children, to them as had built theirselves little shacks right back in the Bush, an' was mostly Tasmanian ticket-o'-leaf men, an' nothin' for nobody to boast on), they used to work some of 'em at fallin' the Bush, an' some at sawin' the timber in the sawpits. An' then, when they'd got enough cut, one o' the craft 'ud come down for it from Port, an' some o' the men 'ud go away in a whaleboat up to Town with it—plenty o' the wood Town's built of grew green once in the Bay; an' then, with the money it fetched, they'd buy stores an' bring down. So the men wasn't so bad off, you see, for they did get a change, once in a while; an' rare old sprees some of them used to have too, don't I know it! when they found theirselves back among faces again, an' talk, an' news, *an'* liquor! But the women, with all the cookin' an' cleanin' an' clothin' to do an' mostly nothin' to do it with: an' they a-grievin' for them they'd left behind, an' scarce ever a letter: an' all the change ever *they* got, just to look from the Bush to the sea an' then back from the sea to the Bush: an' the little children a-comin' an' a-comin', with never no doctor to call;—well, my word! I didn't think of it then, nor understand, but many's the time since I've thought, an' I reckon them women had *pluck*!

'As for us young ones, it was our part to bring in what wood we could for the cookin' (you ever use black-pine bark nowadays? It's *the* thing for bakin'—can't be beat), an' to gather mussels off of the rocks when the tide was low; aye, an' many an' many's the fish I've a-caught an' brought home for dinner from the Point there. There was two winter mornin's I remember, us children found a frost-fish an' brought home. Just a-layin' there on the sand one was, all as *quiet*! for all the world like a long silver sash-ribbon... Eh, I remember I did wish it *was* a sash... wouldn't I ha' got it round me quick if it had been! though a rare sight it would ha' made, to be sure, a-tyin' in a dungaree over-all. But that other fish, we saw that a-comin' in; an' it come in a-leapin', an' a-loopin', and all in a flurry (nobody knows, you know, what fetches 'em ashore; only they comes of a frosty mornin'; nor there ain't nobody as ever catched one with a hook or net, far as I've heard say); an' that one, when we got it home, it was long enough to hang right from the top of our door to the bottom, six foot.

'Then we'd to see, us children, to the gardens. That was easy work, bless you! All you had to do in them days was, scratch up the soil where any logs had been burnt, or that was anyways clear in the Bush, an' put in your potatoes, or pumpkins, or maize, or wheat, or whatever it was, an' up they'd come; there didn't want no manurin' or deep spadin' in that kind soil, I can tell you; an' next year, you could make your garden somewhere else—there was plenty o' room. Then, when the wheat come up, us children had to grind it, in a coffee-mill as we'd brought from board-ship. The bread, it was made from the bran an' all; but, seems to me, there's never any now tastes half so sweet.

'What else had we to eat? Well, there was wild pig in the bush, an' the men 'ud get one now an' again; an' there was plenty o' parrots an' pigeon—ah! them pigeons was good! Father 'ud go out a-shootin' in the Bush sometimes of a Sunday mornin' (they didn't work of a Sunday, an' of course there was no church; only once there was the Bishop, Bishop Selwyn, came—it was he as christened your great-aunt Mary Ann there, in old Martin's barn; but that was later); well, an' I'd go with him, an' sometimes he'd shoot as many as twenty, bless you, or twenty-five. Some he'd give away to the neighbours, an' some we'd stew an' eat right hot—I wouldn't mind havin' some of mother's stewed pigeon to-night for my tea, neither, that I wouldn't! An' as for the rest, mother, she used to put 'em in her big pot, first a layer o' pigeon, an' then a layer o' pig, an' like that, pigeon an' pig, pigeon an' pig, till the end of 'em; then a little water, an' seasonin', an' stew 'em, stew 'em, stew 'em slow an' slow... till when you come to eat 'em cold, there they was all in a jelly, an' *tender*—my word! Autumn, when the black pine berries was ripe, was the best time for pigeon—but not spring, for in spring they'd feed on the *goai** bushes, an' that made

* *Kowhai.*

their flesh all bitter. It seems funny now, don't it? to think that every bit o' butter we saw in them days come from England, but so it was; an' all the salt beef too, which was all the meat, but pig, ever we saw. Once, when supplies was pretty low, we tried porpoise—a steak of it; but there, bless you! I'd as soon eat nothin' at all, an' a great deal sooner; though some o' the men said it was all right. An' once we tried shag—an' never no more *but* the once! They did look so nice too, roasted all brown, an' a-smellin' just as *tasty*; but there, the first mouthful, a' that was the last!—don't *you* never cook no shag an' waste good bastin'!

'Tea an' sugar an' tobacco, an' such things, we'd get from Town as we could, any time the men went up with the timber. When they got back depended on the weather, an' sometimes we'd be pretty near clear out o' everythin', an' it was just borrow from whoever could lend till nobody could, an' then, to wait. We'd make tea out of all kinds of Bush things, *manuka* for choice; an' for tobacco the men would grind up different kinds o' bark; but, bless you, they never seemed to get no satisfaction out o' ne'er a-one an' 'twould be grumble, grumble, grumble amongst 'em until the boat got back—about as good company as a teethin' baby is a baccy-lovin' man without his pipe. Clothes? Well, we'd have a roll o' dungaree down at a time, an' everythin' made from that, pants an' jumpers, an' skirts an' bodies, an' all-round pinnies for us children—I can't remember that we ever wore anythin' else in the summer; I'm sure it was warmer then; I'm sure the climate's changed—without *I* have. On our heads we'd have dungaree hoods because o' the "lawyer" a-catchin' at us in the Bush, an' us children always went barefoot, like the Maoris.

'There isn't a Maori left in the Bay now, as you know—not a full-blooded one. Some they went to the North Island; most is dead… well, well! But in them days there was a pretty big *pa* of 'em back there in the Bush, an' in spite of all poor mother could do, it was my dear delight to get to it. Mother, she was good to 'em, though, mind you! Once she even dressed old Marama's hair up in braids, just like her own—an' can't I see old Marama yet, a-pattin' of her head so proud, an' a-sayin', "All a-same *te Pakeha*, all a-same *te Pakeha*," an' never took it down, bless you, for a week.

'I remember Marama cookin' *hapuka* once. She'd a great iron pot, an' what did she put in first of all but a great heap of this here sow-thistle, an' on top of that the fish, all washed an' scaled, an' then fills up the pot with more sow-thistle an' a little water, an' steams it; an' when it was ready we all sat round on the ground in a circle, an' Marama she tipped the pot right out on the ground in the middle, so that the fish lay on the sow-thistle; an' we all took what we wanted— no forks nor plates nor nothin'—an', my word, it was good! You'd ha' thought the sow-thistle would ha' ruined the taste of everythin', nasty, bitter stuff; but it didn't.

'How them Maoris did use to catch fish too! They was the ones, my word! I've a-seen a Maori man a-layin' down on a rock over the sea with a bare hook in his hand, no bait—an' him a-bendin' over, an' a shoal of fishes a-passin' underneath, an' him a-haulin' of 'em out with this 'ere hook, same as I might spoon dumplin's out of a pot. An' the Maori women too—how I did like to see them women a-catchin' eels! Along in the creek they'd go, with their things tucked up, or off, an' they'd stir up the mud as they went, an' feel along the mud for eels, with a wisp of grass in their hand. An' whenever a woman felt a eel, down she'd stoop in the water, an' slip her hand, with the grass in it for grip, right under the eel—for they're slippy things, them… an' my stars! next minute there'd be that eel a-squirmin' right out there on the bank afore you could say "Snuff," an' the Maori woman a-feelin' with her feet for the next.

'My word, though, didn't some of them sawpit fellows use them poor women bad! There was one of 'em, Roimata (well-named, for it means "Tears") used to live with Black Joe. My! he was a bad one!— an' there he'd knock her about, an' lock her in so's she couldn't get away, an' carry on all sorts, till the poor soul was fair desperate, an' tried to hang herself with a flax rope. But it broke, so it did, an' cut her throat bad in the breakin'. The tumble, an' the sight of her own blood scared her so as to save her; for a-lookin' up an' around an'

all ways for somethin' to help, there she sees the chimney; an' lively
wi' fright, she does what she'd never ha' thought, most-like, o' doin,
else—she scrambles up that chimney, an' out, an' down the other
side, an' comes to mother, all over bruises an' blood (my word! she
was a sight), but anyway, safe from Joe. Mother she kep' her till it was
evenin' an' she could get away to her own people, an' they smuggled
her out o' the Bay, an' Joe never got her again.

'Eh dear! I remember Roimata said a thing that afternoon, though,
as must ha' made mother feel a real Christian to help her after. You
see, the Maori women's ways wasn't just our ways, nor our men
hadn't helped 'em, mostly, to be so; an' while Roimata an' mother
was a-talkin' friendly together that afternoon, Roimata, she says,
quite innocent, "An' how many men," she says, "*you* had?" "Me?
Why, whatever does the woman take me for? Why, one, of course,
an' that my own lawful wedded husband!" cries mother, a-bridlin'
an' a-bristlin' of herself till she didn't look like the same woman—she
was a meek-lookin' woman, mother was, an' pretty too, even to a
Maori taste, it seemed; for Roimata, she puts her head on one side,
an' lookin' at her kind of sly, "Too much the lie!" says she, quite
positive, as if you couldn't hope to take *her* in about it—she knew
better than you, if needful. "E! too much the lie!" she says, an' looked
so sure, that mother she gave up bein' angry all of a sudden an' just
burst out a-laughin'. "The poor heathen!" says mother, as soon as
she could speak, an' ever after that she always spoke of Roimata as
"that poor heathen."

'Yes, that Joe, an' some o' the others, was proper bad lots, so they
was! Poor mother, she went in terror of her life of 'em, at one time;
for they'd get them liquor down from Town, an' there they'd take an'
drink it till it was done (an' they done too, pretty nigh), in a little
rotten shanty near to ours on the shore, that they called "the Old
House at Home." I used to think it wasn't any wonder they'd a-left
Home, if their old houses was really like that; an' mother, she used
to wish more than enough they'd a-stayed there; for the noise they'd
make at night in that quiet place, where mostly there was nothin'

but the lappin' o' the sea, and the morepork callin', you couldn't ha' believed,—an' o' course there was fights as well. The Maoris used to say when they heard them noises, that it was *Taipo* (that's the devil, you know), an' I reckon they was about right.

'Well, but at last, one night after they'd all cleared out, that there "Old House at Home," it got burnt down; an' nobody ever rightly knew how, only them as done it. The men was no-ways daunted, though; soon as ever they could, they gets down more liquor an' puts up another shanty, an' that they christened in raw rum, "The New House at Home." But the very first night of their carousin' in it, there's a note gets thrown in at the door a-tellin' 'em, how, if it didn't behave itself no better than the Old, the New House at Home was a-goin' to be burnt down too—an', my word, if it wasn't! no more than a couple o' nights later. My! the men *was* mad. Why, they even got the constable down from Town, for to see into it—an' a new novelty it must ha' been to most of 'em, I'll warrant, to be playin' hounds with the constable, 'stead o' hare. But, bless you! he never found out nothin' no more than they, an' pretty soon he went back.

'Morris, he'd a-lent them his barn for to house the liquor as had come down from Town with the constable, an' to drink it in too; only you may be sure the drinkin' was quite polite so long as the constable stayed. They was a-reckonin' on a real good spree, though, the night he left, an' there! I declare I could almost feel sorry for them men, it's so hard to 'a counted on a thing as didn't never mean to be there, like that there spree. For no sooner was the constable's boat safe round the Head, than I'm blessed if Morris's barn wasn't found to be on fire, too—just too late to save it—an' the kegs inside of it! Well, that just about settled them men. They begun for to think, like the natives, that *Taipo* was in it; an' they didn't trouble to build 'em no more Houses at Home; 'stead o' that, they begun to drop away out o' the Bay theirselves. By that time, for one thing, you see, the most o' the big timber was down, an' the settlers was beginnin' for to settle straight. We didn't begrudge 'em their journey, you may be sure... An' who did burn down them places really? H'm... Well...

whoever it was knew better than to let a secret like that out in front of their teeth; but between you an' me an' that there doorpost, I've always had a taste of a suspicion that there peace-lovin' *Taipo* was very much the same shape as my dear good mother!

'After them men was gone, the Bay was another place. We'd begun to get on a bit, things was more comfortable, the land was getting clear, an' everyone was friends. It was like one big family. We'd all the same aims an' purposes, you see; an' we all had only each other to look to for help, an' sympathy, an' amusement, an' everythin'. Martin, he had a medicine chest, so he was doctor; an' Burns, he used to read us the Bible of a Sunday, an' do the buryin'—there was a baby or two died. Seems to me, lookin' back, that there wasn't half the spite nor the gossip among us that there is among folk now; maybe it was so much fresh air, as well as so few folk; or else maybe there *was* the gossip, only that I overlook an' disremember it; an' a good thing if I do!

'As the Bush got felled, we sowed grass; till by an' by, all the place begun to get a lighter green, an' stock was bein' brought. Well I remember that first cow—Blackbird was her name—an' Punch, the first bullock—father bought him; an' mother an' me we used to have a sledge an' put him in to bring down firewood—though do you suppose we could get him to go? Not we! He'd go all right when he felt like it, an' when he didn't we just had to wait till he did. It wouldn't do to have Punch an' the sledge with mother an' me for drivers, these days that you want to catch the steamer so quickly. An' the first horse… an' sheep… An' the first lamb! my word, it was a great day for us children when that first little lamb was born. Just you try an' imagine what all them animals meant to youngsters that had been pinned in all their lives, there between them two great spurs of Bush, an' the open sea. Wild pig an' porpoise was about the only big live things, besides men an' women, as we'd ever see; and who could be friends with either o' them? Dogs, indeed, the men had had from the start; but don't I remember my first pussy? Tortoise, she was, with a yellow face…

'Soon, too, we begun to build us better houses; an' pedlars started to come from inland by the new roads cut everywhere through the Bush. By an' by Silas Doubleday (that's Johnny's uncle), he set up a store. My! how mother did use to grumble at his molasses. Next thing was, there come a schoolmaster, an' then, stead o' swimmin', an' fishin', an' gardenin' all day long, as we'd a' used to do, the children had to sit still an' learn—an' a very good thing too. I was a young woman by that time, an' a silly I felt, I can tell you, a-settin' there among the little ones, an' a-learnin', at last, how to cipher an' write—read I always could; mother she'd took care o' that. There was some others my own size, though, that was one comfort; an' well I remember your grandfather (as was to be) a-settin' beside me an' a-helpin' me with "seven times," which I never could remember... eh, them days!...

'Then they built a church. Before that, the parson used to come over from Port, every few months, for to marry, an' christen, and preach us a sermon in Martin's big barn. An' then we started a choir— I used to like that fine! All our organ, to be sure, was for years Tim Rafferty's fiddle, the same as was our brass band on the nights when the moon was our 'lectric light, an' the hard sand of the beach our ball-room floor; but our singin'-hall was big enough, anyway, for it was the whole Bay, an' our benches was the boats—we was always great hands for singin' on the water. Water seems a natural soundin'-glass for song, like it's a lookin'-glass for light. Sounded nice it did, an' felt nice, too, I can tell you! An' often as not, we'd make a picnic of it, as far as the Head rocks there; boil the billy, an' have our tea, an' sing ourselves home by moonlight. I used to like them trips.

'An' then at last there came the first steamer! That made more difference to the Bay than anythin', I do believe; for it hook-an'-eyed the Bay folk an' the world. My word, though, how them natives did holler when that first steamer—the little *Jane Seymour* she were—come into the Bay of a windy mornin'! They'd a-seen 'em go past the Bay's mouth often enough, to be sure; we all had; but they'd never seen one a-comin' straight as a string for the head of the Bay in the teeth of a southerly wind. Made sure, they did, as it was *Taipo* a-comin' for to carry 'em all away; an' they let loose one yell out o' thirty throats, an' then up an' away an' back in the Bush, the quickest things on God's round earth. They always thought as everythin' they didn't understand was *Taipo*; but, mind you, once finish their fright, an' they'd tumble to an' understand pretty quick...

'Ever I tell you that there tale about the pigs? No? Well, it was after I was grown up, but afore I was married, an' it was one year when we had a good lot o' fine big pigs. We had a neighbour, too; Larry O'Neill was his name, an' you can guess his nation; and father an' he was partners that year in pig. Well, Larry, he wanted some pork one day, but what he didn't want was to kill any o' his an' ours; so what does he do, but he hollers out a pum'kin, one o' them long yeller kind, an' cuts slits in the rind, two for eyes, one straight down for nose, an' another for mouth straight across; an' then, at night, he puts a candle inside of this here pum'kin, lights it, an' goes, very soft, up close to the fence of the Maori *pa*; an' there he begins to groan, an' to whine, an' to whimper, an' to screech, an' to make in general the most ungodly noises you ever did hear; an' then, when the natives peep out, scared to death almost already—for you know they didn't dare out ever after dusk for fear of *Taipo*—there was this here horrible face in the pum'kin, all a-lit up, an' a-grinnin' at 'em!

'So they knew there *was* a *Taipo* after them that time for sure, not only havin' heard but seen him; an' the next day some o' the women come down to mother, an' says, did she see that *Taipo* last night? an' to take care o' our pigs because *Taipo* he'd a-gone off with one o' theirs. If they'd a-looked into Larry's house on the way back, they'd a-seen where he'd gone off with it *to*; an' mother she said she never felt so mean in all her born life, an' not a bite o' that pig would she demean herself for to touch, nor yet any of the others—for, after that, whenever Larry felt like fresh pork, he'd up an' play another game o' *Taipo*. Three fine fat pigs he got for nothin' that way, an' goodness knows how many more it might ha' been, but that one mornin', very early, before any of us was up, we heard a great squealin' o' pigs up at the *pa*, an' mother, she says, "I doubt Larry won't get much more Maorified pork, an' a very good thing, too; for they seem to be killing the lot." An' then, while we was a-dressin', we saw their biggest canoe

a-goin' out the Bay, an' "There goes the Maori pigs up to Town," says
mother again.

'But, O dearie me! it wasn't the Maori pigs as had gone to town.
When father went down for to feed 'em, he found it was *ours*! ours,
an' that thief of a Larry's! It seems, the natives they'd tumbled at last
to the *Taipo* business, an' this here was the way they was a-settlin' the
fresh pork bill, an' a-havin' their little joke all in one— they'd stole all
our pigs before we was up, killed 'em in our very ears, an' sent 'em up
to town afore our very eyes, an' that at the rate o' ten to three. Larry
he laughed fit to split his sides when he saw it all, an' father, though
he was a bit vexed—an' I don't wonder—he couldn't help but laugh
too... Mother she didn't. Anybody say anythin' to the natives about
it? No, how could they? But I can tell you one thing though—*Taipo*
didn't trouble the *pa* much after that.

'Well, well! the *pa* itself is gone now, an' there's the cheese-factory
in its place; an' you've church every week, an' a public hall an' library,
an' a couple o' stores; an' a steamer a-callin' every other day for to
bring you mails from Town, an' the mornin' paper, an' baker's bread,
my word! an' to carry you off for to see your grannies any time you've
a mind. Civilisation on tap, as you may say. But I'm not a-goin' to
give in to it, for all that, as you've a-got all the meat while we had all
the shell. There's many a worse thing to be had in this world than
light hearts, an' good nature, an' neighbourliness; besides, we've all of
us grown up tough an' hearty, an' done our day's work in the world.

'But yet I'm not a-goin' to say as we had all the best of it either.
The want o' too much jam on your bread don't make everythin' else
sweet, so far as I can see; an' ours was a rough life, an' a narrow. It's
good to think as the children can be taught. It's good to think as the
men needn't now to drop asleep all wore out, or to stay awake fit for
nothin' but liquor, after the tough day's work o' sawin' or burnin';
an' to know that the women can have their washin' machines an'
their sewin' machines, an' stoves—yes, an' their pianos, too, an' their
time to think as there's somethin' else in the world besides children
an' the Bay.

'Yes, I reckon there's a good word to be said for these days, as well as them days—an' for them as well as these. Well! Well! but for my part I must own as I'm glad it was in them I mostly lived. It's good to be in at the sowin' o' seed that's bound to grow, be it cabbage, or a country. Look now, an' see, does the kettle boil? For there's your mother a-comin' up the street.'

## Aboard a Coasting Schooner

Among the many coastal steamers which line the wharves of any fair-sized port in New Zealand, there will generally be found two or three specimens of another class of vessel, less imposing to the eye, but to the fancy perhaps even more endearing—I mean the coasting schooners. Upon a sea renowned for its storms, and off a coast that bristles with dangers, these adventurous and often beautiful little boats—sea-butterflies in appearance, sea-housewives in utility, sea-heroines in pluck—flit continually back and forth, and succeed in carrying, and with a degree of punctuality surprising under the circumstances, cargoes of commodities, passengers, and news, to the tiny settlements or single homesteads which they serve as flying bridges between solitude and the world.

Towards the close of a golden summer's evening, now several years ago, one such schooner, the *Tikirau* (82, Captain Fletcher), pushed and panted her way down Auckland harbour, her white wings fully spread, and her little oil-engine resolutely, for once, at work. She had done exactly the same thing many and many a time before, for she was a boat with a regular trade-route of her own; and more than once had I enviously admired from the shore the gliding of her exquisite white hull and snowy canvas, and her air—that air which belongs of right to every small craft going forth to front great seas and skies, but which always seemed to hang doubly glamorous about the *Tikirau*—of bravery and adventure and romance.

This time, however—*this* time—aha! there was a difference. No longer was she mere, remote, cold 'she.' No longer must I wistfully watch her from the 'steady, unendurable land.' Oh, triumph, no! From a snug, if somewhat narrow, niche upon her own deck was I this time proudly regarding her; I, yes, actually I too, was aboard!

All the way down to her southernmost limit, all the way back to Hauraki, she and I—we—we, warm *we*, if you please—were going a-coasting together! Witness of the bravery I was to be, sharer of the adventure, *in* the romance. Hurrah!

She was a full boat that evening. As I looked along her deck (flush fore and aft), I wondered if ever a portion of space had been more thoroughly packed. There were the fixtures, to begin with, the galley amidship, freshly painted to an appetising pink-and-white; the wheel; and, right aft, just forward of the wheel, the low oblong roof of the 'house,' with its microscopical cabins and nutshell of a saloon. And then there were the extras—and everything that term included, it would take pages to recount. From bow to stern, to begin with, the deck was overlaid with a consignment of yellow-brown *kauri* timber, the uppermost tier of which was fairly on a level with her rail; and on top of this were heaped and piled, lashed and carefully secured under a great tarpaulin, a multitude of queer-looking lumps, whose nature it was far from easy to determine; together with a quantity of casks, kegs, and oil-tins, many wooden cases, and a boat for some settler on the coast—rurally converted, this last, for the time being, into an agreeable vignette of barn-door life at sea; for the bow and body of it were richly green with fine fat cabbages and cauliflowers, while the stern was shared by a black, red-ribboned cat (passenger), and a rooster in a coop. There was also a lady-like camellia, in a pot, displaying its glossy leaves just forward of the 'house,' and all but concealing a certain little dark gap in the deck, and a miniature funnel close by. The gap, I found afterwards, was the entrance to a tiny engine-room; the funnel took one by the nose with a double-distilled breath of benzine, and explained itself on the spot as belonging to the little auxiliary oil-engine. It was early in the days of engines aboard such ships as the *Tikirau*, and ours was something of an adventurous innovation… To tell the truth, there were times when it was *all* adventure! Lack of pretence was its abounding virtue, and seldom, indeed, so long as I knew it, did it dissemble, by any false alacrity in starting, its deep reluctance to proceed. On the starboard beam, a beautiful whaleboat painted white, like the rest of the ship, swung from her davits; fore- and main-masts shot up burnished in the evening light, hoisted head-sails, fore-sail and main, caught and held its gold. With these, and the orderly confusion of the rigging, the very air above the deck appeared as fully occupied as the space below—which, in addition to all the inanimate objects already catalogued, found room too, as we dropped down the harbour, for the entire ship's company, eight all told: for a little knot of passengers, respectfully keeping out of the way in the neighbourhood of the wheel; and, really to end the list at last, for a satin tabby-cat (on top of the galley), a white fox-terrier, a black retriever, and a couple of very plump pups—rioting, these last, among the men's feet, and acquiring with howls some of the rudiments of discipline.

My fellow-passengers, it soon appeared, included a schoolmaster and his wife, returning to their charge, a native school; a storekeeper and *his* wife homeward-bound after a trip to town; and the rather numerous offspring of both couples. The *Tikirau* was their customary conveyance, and they all seemed quite at home.

'Not too much room, is there?' responded one of the ladies good-naturedly when, in shifting my position, I had to apologise for standing upon her feet as well as my own. 'We shall be pretty snug below, I reckon, but it's only a couple of days or so, is it, after all? How far down are you going? Our crowd gets off at the first port.'

'Pretty snug,' we certainly were when it came to 'turning in.' Indeed, how we actually were all stowed away, I cannot now conceive. But it was managed somehow; the *Tikirau* was a resourceful ship—and not resourceful only. She carried aboard of her, besides cargo and crew, a spirit of cordiality and easy comradeship, of hearty and active willingness to make the best of things, that won over into cheerfulness and 'roughitability' the most fastidious, and translated every drawback into a joke. The lights had begun to sparkle and twinkle at our heels and on either shadowy shore, before we reached the Head. We rounded it—and suddenly the city was obliterated, the lights were gone, and, in the deepening dusk, space grew about us.

The engine, too, was stopped, the sea-silence fell, and, amid the silence and the darkness and the ever-widening space, the little *Tikirau* stole ghostlike out to sea. The voyage had begun.

I fell asleep listening to the silence, but during the night I heard from the next cabin a child's voice, pleading pitifully for the ship to stop, 'an' I'll *walk* home, mummy, I truly will!' The breeze with which we had started was, in fact, freshening considerably; and when morning came, and we staggered, those of us who could, out upon a very slantwise deck, we learned that it was blowing half a gale already, and about to blow some more; that the coast hereabouts was too dangerous to be trifled with, and that we were already running for shelter to an island close by.

It was a wild, magnificent scene. The sun was as brilliant as the wind was furious, there was not one cloud in all the great, shining sky, the sea was a flashing battlefield where the richest, most gorgeous blue imaginable strove for mastery with the brightest and most glittering white; and over the riotous waves, and before the invigorating wind, the little *Tikirau* was flying spiritedly along among a regular, or rather irregular, network of islands—some mere pinnacles and spits of black volcanic rock, bursting out, as it were, from the windy blue amid sharp outbursts of foam: others running out upon it, in long necks and headlands, capped with tawny turf enough to pasture a few wild goats, and low, shaggy Bush: while others again boldly reared themselves up, and braved its azure on-rush with radiant rose-coloured cliffs. All alike were uninhabited; and for a fancy that loved adventure, as well as for an eye that loved colour and light, a better playground would have been hard to find. Then all of a sudden we ran round a bluff, and found ourselves in a small, sickle-shaped bay, deeply sunk between the horns of two high promontories, rimmed with snowy sand, and enclosing a shining crescent of smooth, sapphire water, which looked as though no breath of wind had stolen across it for a week.

There we anchored, and there we stayed all day, for the gale outside continued unabated. Inland, the cliffs ran up into great boulder-strewn hills, sparsely covered with short turf, and low *manuka*-scrub; and here, fossicking about for the rough-looking lumps of what, when scraped, revealed itself as *kauri*-gum (for *kauri* forest once covered all these barren isles), and setting the boulders to race each other down-hill—oh, the glorious pace they put on!—we managed to amuse ourselves well enough. From the Captain's point of view, however, the delay was less enjoyable, and the old school-master too, Mr Quin, was already 'behind his time' and anxious to get back to duty. He was, however, a gentle old man, and blessed with a remarkable talent for equanimity—the credit of which, if the crew's demure report was to be trusted, was partly at least due to Mrs Quin's equally remarkable talent for giving it exercise; so presently he observed: 'A bad start, my long experience has led me to believe, frequently makes a good finish. And, after all, what a sad pity it would be, supposing we were never granted any opportunity in life for being philosophical!'

Cheerfulness is, perhaps, one of the very most desirable qualities a shipmate can possess. One felt obliged to Mr Quin. And his wife was cheerful too, never mind what her other proclivities may have been. A heartening thing it was to see that worthy woman making the best of it at meal times—'Sure, I've no teeth an' no appetite, an' a wee bit of pitaty is all I can be 'atin'... an' just a toothful of cabbage, Mr Black. Eh? No; a little bit more than that—an' a crust of bread, Quin; an' mind you, now, for you cut the last too thin for annythin' solider than a speerit— an' now, Cap'n, I'll just be troublin' you for the least littlest taste more mutton, if you plase—wid a lump o' that fat to it. Sure I've not much appetite; I have not.'

We got away again during the evening, and the next day made a good run past a stretch of the coast where the *Tikirau* did not trade. That was a capital day. The wind was now right aft, and we sailed 'goose-wing,' the foresail swung out to port, the main to starboard, and the vessel shooting buoyantly forward upon an even keel, with a joyous, exhilarating motion. The boom of the mainsail thus obligingly out of the way, the house-roof suggested itself as a pleasant point of vantage, elevated, and uncrowded; and there luxuriously within a coil of rope I sat for most of the day, and revelled in my mercies. It was a world of motion—splendid, unimpeded, exultant; only to be aware of it was power; to share it was to be ten times alive. The clean wind blew and blew, and the clouds raced before it; the great merry waves leapt high into the air, as they came chasing after us, and shoals of porpoises rollicked along in the bright clear water on either side of the vessel as though they recognised in her a playmate—now vigorously rolling their bright black bulks in and out the sparkling surface, now like a company of pale green meteors streaming swiftly below and through it. ('With all our knowledge we don't come near their power,' old Mr Quin mused aloud, as he leaned over the side to watch them.) And, with all these forces of Nature, the little *Tikirau*, as she hastened along upon her routine business, with her humble and homely cargo and us humdrum folk aboard, seemed somehow freely to be one. Elemental, spontaneous, gleeful, she too appeared; she was an incarnate joy, a sea-spirit of delight, a spark of perennial and quenchless activity, somehow encased in canvas and iron and timber; she was—I don't know what she was! but she looked like a bit of Nature; she behaved like a live thing; she felt like a friend, and I loved her! Ships are like horses and people—they have a very definite personality of their own, readily to be felt by those susceptible in such matters. And, of all the ships that I have ever known, the little *Tikirau* stands out in my fond remembrance as easily the kindliest, the happiest, and the sweetest-natured.

The day after this, we made our first port, and there my fellow-passengers were landed, all except the Quins. It was a picturesque little place. Mountains, clothed to the summit with thick virgin Bush, ran in a long, unbroken wall parallel with the shore, from which they were separated by a narrow stretch of tableland, treeless and low. The sea-line of this stretch was broken by the jutting forth of a small promontory, above which the white spire of a little church, a noticeable landmark, rose up from among the low clustered roofs of a native settlement. Tumbled fragments of black rock studded the foot of the promontory; the wind had fallen, and the sun, although gradually brightening, was veiled in haze; it was a morning of mauve and lavender, and the water lifted and sank in long even glassy swells, so pale as to be almost colourless.

While the whaleboat was making her first trip ashore with passengers and luggage, the rest of the crew busied themselves in preparing the next load, and the ship showed, so to speak, another side of herself, and turned, as she swung comfortably at anchor, into a market-place. The hatches were off, and all kinds of household riches began to come up out of the holds—white bags of flour, brown ones of sugar, boxes of soap and candles, cases of drapery and provisions, and 'sundries' of all sorts, shapes, and sizes. The mate's voice came up thin and distant from the main hold, deep in the depths of which he was singing out the various items as the winch hauled them up; while on deck, the purser, seated upon a cask, kept a careful tally. Everybody, I observed, engineer and cook included, was 'bearing a hand' in this business of discharging; it was never, aboard that boat, natural to be so haughty and select as to stick to your own job only.

Some of the timber had already been lashed into a raft, and this, presently, was vigorously shoved over the well-greased rail, and left to drift ashore. The faint sunshine brought out all the mellow hues of the wetted planks as they rose and fell upon the waves; it dwelt pleasantly upon the green 'garden' in the boat, polished the camellia leaves, slightly lit the masts as they swayed to and fro, and painted to pale gold the mainsail lying heaped in its lazy-jacks, and the fore- and head-sails drooping in gathered bunches as one sees them in the old sea-pictures. Overhead the shrouds and ratlines rocked, sharply black, upon the gentle grey sky; and the holds at one's feet presented pits of a rich darkness. A little column of blue wood-smoke streaming up from the galley brought the Bush out to sea; Tim, the cook, splitting *manuka* for his stove at an odd moment of leisure, and the two pups fighting for a bone—white Floss and black Darkie had hilariously gone ashore in the boat—lent an air of real domesticity to the scene. But, ah! all the while, underneath, swung, heaved, breathed the joyous instability!

At the captain's invitation, I went ashore with him in the 'second boat,' just to have a 'look round.' We were greeted by an eager assemblage—all native, with the single exception of our late shipmate, the store-keeper, who was watching the delivery of his goods—and all very smiling and gay. The arrival of the *Tikirau* was the event of the month, for no other vessel traded to this port, and a track along the coast was its only other link with civilisation. The sight of all these brown, bright-eyed faces waiting beside the surf carried one's fancy clean back to the days of Captain Cook; and nothing, at a little distance, was easier than to imagine ourselves the original *pakeha* explorers of this shore. But the moment we landed, yesterday took to its heels, and pale fancy proved nothing of a rival to robust reality—robust, and lively!

Tall, well-built men (the Maori of this district is among the finest of his race), all in European dress: women in loose, fluttering garments of indigo, pink, or white, with the blue tattoo (is it not really rather becoming?) beneath the lower lip, a silk handkerchief over the rich, rippling hair, and rosy bloom beneath the golden-brown of their cheeks: young girls, lads, children of all ages:—the whole crowd dashed at once upon their visitors with the loudest and friendliest of welcomes. Cries of the all-embracing *Tenakoutou* (Here you all are!), of the discriminating *Tenakoe* (Here thou art!), came musically from every mouth, and there was much enthusiastic shaking of hands. The captain, it was instantly evident, was a popular and universally trusted visitor, and everybody who was anybody began at once to pour into his ear (poor man, he needed dozens, and large at that!) tidings of some unexampled need for *huka*, *hopi*, and *paraoa* (melodious Maorifications of *sugar*, *soap*, and *flour*), or inquiries as to some private consignment, such as a pipe, a walking-stick, or a hat with flowers in it; while the rest, biding their time, occupied themselves meanwhile in talk and laughter with the boat's crew, vociferous comments upon the goods already landed, and a minute examination of each package.

Several horses, with remarkably long tails, stood patiently waiting beside a *puriri* tree a little way along the beach—the owners had ridden in from their scattered homes at the first word of the *Tikirau*'s approach; many of the women squatted in conversational groups upon the sand, and puffed at short black pipes; the younger men helped to bear the packages up the beach, the elders looked on and gave advice, and there was much excitement on the part of many dogs, of course including ours. The little *Tikirau*, riding so peacefully out yonder, had sent ashore quite a stir.

It was good to see that, with scarcely an exception, the children seemed to be in the best and bonniest of health; they were well-formed, well-grown, and plump. But among the grown men and women the ravages of tuberculosis were, alas! only too evident. One face I vividly remember. It was that of an old man. Pitifully emaciated, wrapt in a thick blanket for all the sunshine, which was by this time cloudless, and leaning over a stick, he stood a little aside from his active, eager neighbours and with hazel eyes paled by mortal sickness gazed wistfully, not at them, not at the bounty-bearing *Tikirau*, but away out over the empty sea to the void horizon—and beyond. Still in life, already he was not of it.

While the unloading, the squaring of accounts, and other general business thus proceeded on the beach, I took a tour round the settlement, Te Kaha by name. It was an excellent example of the type general upon that coast, therefore a brief description of it will be economical and save words about the rest. Its public buildings were three in number—the school-house, of the usual anti-picturesque appearance, the landmark church already mentioned, bare and clean, and the native hall or meeting-house, which was no bad type of the native race in its present transitional condition; for its roof was of grey galvanised iron, while the barge-boards of its deep eaves were richly carved with the characteristic Maori patterns, and crowned by a very fine *teko-teko* (carved figure), with the customary grimacing face, protruding tongue of defiance, and gleaming *pawa*-shell eyes. Inside, matters were more purely native. Panels of scroll-work painted in harmonious dark-blue, crimson, and white, brightened the single, long, barn-like interior; rolls of mats and blankets indicated its use at night as a community bedroom; hanks of dressed flax glistened like white silk upon the walls, and a couple of pleasant-faced women, careless, for some cause, of the ship's arrival, were busily weaving a mat. Even here, too, however, there were incongruous traces of the *pakeha*. Between two of the panels, there hung a *Graphic* picture of one 'Adeliza,' highly coloured, golden-tressed, low-bodiced, very tight-laced; several cloth jackets richly trimmed with jet hung beside it, and a large swing looking-glass, such as more generally stands upon a dressing-table, decorated the floor in the neighbourhood of the two women and emphasised, slanderously, I trust, the proportions of the passing foot.

As to the private dwellings, they were the ordinary *whares*, of varying size, standing in separate plots of ground, with palings of brown *punga* (tree-fern stem) between them, and over the palings very brightly striped blankets flung forth, most sensibly, for an airing. Streets, in our sense of the word, there were none; but little paths of grass meandered between some of the fences, and provided, no doubt, all the access needed among neighbours so near. By the sighting of the *Tikirau* the little town had been 'emptied of its folk that pious morn.' Peace and silence brooded above the *whares*. Blue-gums, willows, and poplars here and there stood sentinel over the low, smokeless roofs; there were rose-trees as well as potato-blossom in some of the garden patches; while, beyond the outermost palisade of the *pa*, broad, fenceless fields of tasselling maize spread away towards the forest-dark hills, and before the sweet blues and purples of the now sunny sea laid an unshadowed strip of sweet and lively green.

During the afternoon we made and worked another port—a little grassy bay this time, containing in itself no buildings at all, except a kind of open barn stacked with golden maize cobs; but tapping a trade district, and possessing some special advantages. One side of it ran out into a curious little peninsula, of the usual black volcanic rock, which terminated in an island, and made of the bay a natural harbour, familiarly known aboard as the 'Boarding-house.' That very same night proved its virtues; within the breakwater we lay snug, though the wind had swung round and was blowing strong from an undesirable quarter.

Morning brought with it no moderation; it was useless to think of getting out. 'So much the better,' one of the men observed to me in an undertone. 'Like peaches? 'Cause this is the shop for them.' And, accordingly, after breakfast nearly all of us were off ashore, and kits and sacks went with us. I have no space, and I should like to imagine that I had the power, to describe that rare ramble. We peered down from the low cliffs through black boughs of *pohutukawa* trees, still starred here and there with blood-red blossoms, upon the great, green, glassy combers that rolled majestically inshore, to slip suddenly over, as they neared the yellow sand, in long crashing waterfalls of snow. We scrambled through undergrowth, fought through 'lawyer,' waded through fern, jumped little creeks, apostrophised supple-jacks, and from time to time kept coming out upon some unexpected open glade. Green grass would spread it with the softest carpet, and in the middle of the grass there would be a tree or two, perhaps a little grove of trees, with the rosy gold of ripe peaches glowing between the leaves.

The early missionaries, I was told, had planted these trees, which now, in the little clearings from which all other sign of human occupancy has long since departed, still flourish faithfully, and bear fruit. 'Missionary,' in the North Island is frequently an alternative spelling for 'sweet-brier,' which is a pest. As a matter of mere justice, therefore, I am glad to take this opportunity of pointing out that it can also spell 'peaches,' which are not. We found apple-trees, too, figs, and plums along the coast, all planted by the same long-quiet hands, and grapes, I was told, later in the year might be had also for the gathering.

One very pleasant half hour of the afternoon was spent in repairing our friend Mrs Quin, the valiant struggle of whose fourteen stone or so through the Bush had left behind her, in addition to a very fair wake, a considerable portion of petticoat. Our implements were but plain; they consisted of a sail-needle, some blue worsted with which it happened to be threaded, some green flax (throw a copper into the fountain of Trevi if you wish to revisit Rome: if you would come back home to New Zealand, sew a garment with green flax), the mate's fingers, and every one's ungrudging advice; but the effect they produced was striking, and it gave us great satisfaction, in spite of the heroine's scathing 'Sure, 'tis a walking piece o' patchwork wid a bite out of ut I do be lookin'—no offence to ye, Mr Black, for I know ye done your best!' Finally, we harnessed Floss and Darkie to our kits of peaches, and raced them home to the whaleboat across the soft sand of the beach. That was a very good day.

By the morning following the wind had shifted a point or two, and the skipper decided to put out. The engine was accordingly started, sail set, the anchor hove in, and we had just got beyond our break-water, and well into the tumble outside, when, at one and the same moment, the wind failed, and our imp of an engine stopped dead.

So there we were, with all that spread of canvas, and our getting-out just as far advanced as to have brought us beyond shelter—help-less, and extremely close to a shore that, of a sudden, had completely lost all charm. It was an anxious moment. 'If worrying would help, I would worry,' murmured gentle Mr Quin, 'but it won't; so I don't.' Far less 'philosophical' were the rest of us, I fear; and the maker of that engine ('Engine? Darning-machine, you mean!' snorted one of the men) must have had more anxious moments than one—many more—if only half the wishes then expressed so frankly on his behalf came true. Mrs Quin was eloquent for a long time; then I suppose her conscience pricked her, for she finished with the following com-fortable combination of 'pious' with 'natural' feeling. 'Oh, lave the poor man to God! Isn't that what my mother advised herself when a mean skunk of a fellow went an' killed the wan little goat on her, that was all she had, bless her! to feed us childer wid? And widin the year, was there wan baste in all that gintlemin's paddick but had died? There was not. Now!'

The boat meanwhile had been sent out with a kedge anchor, by means of which the *Tikirau* was soon warped back to a safe position; and this was no sooner accomplished than the engine, of course, started work. It puffed us forth once more into the wind with the greatest good-will, apparently, in the world, and seemed ready to go on for days. But as soon as we were well out, instead of stopping us, I am glad to say the darning-machine got stopped itself, and away with all her might (somehow, one never thought of the engine as being part of her might, or indeed part of her in any way), flew the *Tikirau*, bounding and dancing, swinging and leaping over the great blue hills of water like a wild thing rejoicing in liberty.

That afternoon we were able at last to land the loudly thankful Quins—Mrs Quin's expressions having a deeper depth than we understood at the time, for among her various bundles and kits she was slyly conveying ashore with her ('convey, the wise it call') the greater portion of our harvest of peaches. Peace be with her! On our way back she made amends after her own fashion with a cake—made after her own fashion, also; it must have had pounds of butter in it. 'That's the worst of Ma Quin—never no reasonableness with her,' Mr Black observed, on getting clear of his first and only mouthful. 'Got a tongue o' leather that'll never wear out, an' yet a heart o' gold; do hanythink for you if you was sick—an' then go and make you sick with truck like this 'ere. Got no moderation, the old lady hasn't.' Well, and she was in consequence much more interesting than some people one meets, who have nothing else! I missed 'Ma Quin.'

After they went I was the only woman aboard, and remained so for nearly all the rest of the trip. People have sometimes asked me whether I did not find the position awkward. Never; not a bit! there was nothing to make it so. The crew were a steady, respectable set of men—upon that point the captain was particular; I never heard a foul word from any one of them all the time I was aboard; and the *Tikirau* carried no liquor. 'I suppose, then, you were treated as a kind of princess?' has been sometimes an alternative suggestion, to which, 'Not a bit!' is again the answer. No; I was treated just as an ordinary woman is ordinarily treated in New Zealand by her male fellow-citizens—that is, with a frank friendliness; respectful because self-respecting, easy without familiarity, and probably due, partly at any rate, to the political equality of the sexes—certainly not in the very least endangered by it. Nothing, perhaps, in all New Zealand intercourse is more marked and more charming than this trait. A princess aboard the *Tikirau*? No, thank you! I was something infinitely more to be envied—an equal, a comrade, a shipmate; to be freely talked to, listened to, helped, confided in or laughed at, as occasion demanded—And have I ever enjoyed myself more?

A word or two now as to the individual members of the ship's company. Skipper first, of course. Captain Fletcher was a short, wiry man, with a beard already turning grey—for a seaman ages early as to looks; essentially active both in mind and body, and in manner rather reserved, although he was excellent company when you knew him. As a man, he bore a well-merited reputation for kindliness, integrity, and, best of all, scrupulous justice; as a seaman, he had often been proved both skilful and wary. 'Never knew the old man's equal for dodging weather,' was an approving sentence that I often heard aboard the *Tikirau*. He had an extreme dislike to being better off in any way than his men; and, to the scandalisation of Tim, the cook-steward, who considered such a state of things 'unnatural,' afterguard and foremast hands upon that democratic vessel took their meals together; nor would the skipper even permit, to Tim's extra disgust, the least additional luxury at his end of the table. He often worked side by side with his crew; and I have known him fret at having to set one of the hands to do what he would have disliked doing himself. At the same time, so safely and completely, other things being equal, is position secured by character, he was in every conceivable way the master of his ship, and possessed, moreover, the unqualified respect of every one aboard. '*When* he likes,' too, I was informed, 'the old man can say *what* he likes, an' mean it, too, and no mistake about it!' I could say a good deal more concerning Captain Fletcher; and I only do not say it because his eye may possibly fall upon these words, and I have no desire to endanger, by falling foul of that stern modesty which is another of his characteristics, a friendship won during that trip upon the *Tikirau*, and, I am proud to believe, flourishing still.

Next, Mr Black, the mate—a square-set little cockney, rough in appearance, somewhat gruff of speech, all at sea as to his 'h's' and of a nature most hot-hearted and impulsive. 'Jolly funny,' I learned, could Mr Black be, when he 'had a full cargo aboard'; and I did not doubt it, although happy to be spared the entertainment. On the other hand, he was easily the most domesticated sailor I have ever met. Without the faintest hesitation, it appeared, he had at a week's notice dashed into marriage with the widowed mother of a large family, and to use his own words, 'hadn't never looked back on it neither.' 'W'en we was spliced, wot's more, we 'adn't no more than a one arf crown between us!' he added, and seemed to think this was the crowning triumph.

'Most imprudent!' said I.

'Imprudent?' said he. 'Tell you w'at. That's twelve year ago, that is, an' I on'y wishes it was twenty-four.' The heartiness of his tone explained these somewhat ambiguous words as a noble tribute to Mrs Black. 'Now, you jest look a-here, an' berlieve *me*,' he went on with emphasis. 'Merriage, w'y—merriage is orl *right*, I tell yer!'

'Hold on a bit! there's two sides to every plate, chum,' objected Tim, who was also a married man. 'Look at all the worries you get, an' the responsibilities, an' the bills, an the kiddies gettin' sick—I got one sick now—an'—'

'An' w'en yer gits 'ome, the pair o' sleeves wiv two harms in 'em roun' yer neck. An' that's worf it hall!' finished Mr Black, with feeling.

Upon my spinster liberty he was wont to comment with a bitter disapproval. He only scowled when I suggested with a sigh, that the otherwise blameless existence of Mrs Black had now blasted my prospects for ever; and used scathingly to refer to me as 'the man-hater'—most unfairly, for I liked Mr Black.

Mr Scott, the old engineer, was hale and hearty, rosy and smiling, but somewhat taciturn and very deaf. Intercourse with him was difficult in any case, for at meals his plate received his undivided attention, and the remainder of his waking hours appeared to be spent in silent communion with his sphinx of an engine, which he never left, whether she were working or not. She had, as previously hinted, not the sweetest breath in the world; so that there was point in Mr Anstruther's suggestion that her adorer must have an affection of the nose as well as of the heart.

Mr Anstruther was the purser, and a good foil in many ways to old Mr Scott; for he was a sprightly and active young man, the impersonation of light-heartedness and good-humour, always ready for anything, work or play, and a great hand at making and appreciating practical jokes, against himself if occasion demanded—he was not particular. The puppies adored Mr Anstruther. Cats have no sense of humour, and poor Tib did not.

Of the foremast hands the *Tikirau* carried three; Phil, Tom and Fritz. Tom was steady and sturdy; a silent, fair-haired fellow, and one of the best workers aboard. Phil was tall and dark, and loved a jest; he was now making his last trip down the coast—as a seaman, at least; for on the death of a relative he had lately 'come into a bit of land,' and intended to turn farmer. He was a good-natured, friendly fellow, but everybody has his limit, and poor Phil's shared his watch, wore a stout Teutonic form, and answered to the name of Fritz. None of us, I think, knew Fritz very well; he had what is known as 'a queer temper.' I ventured one day to ask him about his friends in the old country. 'Fräulein,' he replied, almost it seemed to me with sour satisfaction, 'I haf not one friend in de vorld.' 'Won't choke nobody to swallow *that*,' was Phil's comment, when he heard this sad statement. The pair were continually at logger-heads. The last time I heard of Fritz, he, too, had quitted the sea, had got married to a portly Maori dame with some land of her own, and, like Phil, had turned farmer. What a frightful thing it would be if those two farms touched!

Last of all, though by no means least important, comes Tim, the cook-steward. Tim was a half-caste, and a picturesque creature, full of contradictions and contrasts. To begin with, he had the physique of a warrior—over six feet tall he was, and broad in proportion—a noble figure of a man; yet he spent his days contentedly in housewifely dealings with pots and pans, and within quarters so narrow that I used to watch for his entrances and exits to see how he managed them. Then he had a very violent temper, very ready to be roused. 'Ought to have been on deck a bit earlier,' I was told one morning, 'and seen old Tim a-kicking his bread-sponge round the deck, because it hadn't rose.' Yet at the same time no one aboard, not even Mr Anstruther, could more positively scintillate with good humour, nor could any one ever be gentler or more patient with women, children, and dumb animals. Easily elated, again, by some very little thing, he was equally capable of enduring fits of depression. 'I'd a sister once,' he told me; 'she was my mainstay—it was before I married—and she died. Straight off on the bust I went, and drank for seven solid months after.' Blessedly clean about his work was Tim, and a really clever cook, too, and proud of his job. Much of our domestic harmony aboard the *Tikirau* was probably due to him; for although we were soon 'down to tins and salt tucker,' and our meals were simple, as all meals at sea anyway ought to be, yet they were both nourishing and varied, and always interesting.

Oh! those meals aboard the *Tikirau*! They have not lost their relish yet. I have but to close my eyes, and the whole scene comes back to me—that little, artless saloon, fairly filled by its long centre table, with the swing tray of glasses above, and the filter in one corner: the sweet, bright air and sunshine gushing freely through the open skylight, and down the two or three steps of the companion—interrupted there, however, at times, by the massive form of Tim descending with a load of steaming dishes, or that tea-can of phenomenal size—and, round the table, all our expectant, sunburnt, shining faces, and eyes bright with the genuine sea-swing.

I can see once more the Captain at the head of that family table, gravely attentive to his paternal task of distribution; old Mr Scott, equally absorbed in the sacred duties of consumption; Tom, his fair hair brushed carefully into a verandah above his bashful eyes; Fritz, chin to plate, silently ladling in enormous mouthfuls, *more Germanico*; Mr Black, putting into his dealings with his dinner the same heartiness and dispatch which had secured him Mrs Black; Mr Anstruther, brimming over with some humorous nonsense or other: and Phil's brown eyes readily responding to the joke. Yes, indeed! Our plates were not of porcelain; we drank from mugs, and there was no butter-knife; the tablecloth (yes, we had a tablecloth, boiled once a week in a kerosene-tin, hung on a backstay to dry, and ironed while yet a little damp, by the primitive process of being folded underneath a locker cushion and sat upon daily until wanted), our tablecloth lacked gloss perhaps, and our *menu*, as I have said, was limited, and strictly of a sea-going description: but not for the very choicest and most delicately served banquet ashore would I have exchanged one of those hearty reunions. 'Aha! *you* know how to take the lee-side of the duff, I see,' Mr Black was wont to say in friendly approval of my excellent appetite. Alas! I would be content to take but the weatherside, if it might only be again aboard the genial, the congenial *Tikirau*!

But now to get back to the trip. The same day that we landed the Quins, we succeeded, by a bit of rare good luck in the matter of wind, in rounding the chancy, or rather, unchancy, headland, that makes a sharp angle in that part of the coast-line—Cape Runaway, namely; and ran, just at nightfall, into Hicks Bay, a small, deep indentation upon its farther side. Here we had a surprise, and a pleasant one, for the riding-lights of no fewer than four other small vessels twinkled through the twilight, shot streamers of gold down through the quiet water, and lent to this remote and lonely inlet the cheerful and homelike appearance of a peopled port. The men named these boats readily from their rig. 'That's Peters in the *Resolution*; an' that's the *Konini* next, an' the *Coronation*—ought to ha' been in Auckland days ago; an' the little 'un she's the *Aorere*. No'therly bound, all of 'em, an' put in here for shelter. Visitin' cards in the cabin soon, you'll see.'

And, sure enough, the *Tikirau*'s anchor was scarcely down before the plash of oars resounded alongside, and the calling had begun. Our little saloon was shortly refurnished with a tableful of quite new faces, and the evening sped away like a shot in animated discussions concerning weather, trade and—engines.

Just before sunrise next morning, while we were loading our first boat, one after another the rest all slipped past us, out upon their homeward way, for the wind had come fair. Hicks Bay is perhaps the most picturesque spot on all that picturesque coast; and a lovely sight it was that morning. A tawny, grass-grown promontory ran out upon the sea to our right, the opposite barrier was a tumble of black rocks and Bush, and the head of the bay was formed by lofty mountains, covered almost to the water's edge with thick virgin forest. As at Te Kaha, a little white church stood out upon the shore with very precise distinctness against this dark background, and the grey, silken sea was sprinkled by the white sails of the escaping craft. Everything was clear, almost curiously clear, in the still, sober atmosphere. Then suddenly, from the sharp-ruled sea-line eastward, leapt the bright round forehead of the sun, and the daily miracle of light was wrought! Everything came instantly *alive*. The clearness was coloured now, the cleanness polished; visibility was radiance, movement became manifest and shone. The awakening world opened its eyes, and there was a laugh in them; all life drew a deeper breath. The breeze freshened. The ripples that ran shoreward before wind and sun were now of a lively blue, and crisped and ruffled with gold. The wide free air and sky were bright as gems—almost too bright; ashore, the black solidity of the Bush was broken and quickened into green tree-tops of a hundred tones, glossy *karakas* twinkled above the rocks, and the grave little white church smiled. About the sparkling bay, silvery sea-swallows now flashed and darted, and those four homely coasters running out with the wind became four visions of most aerial beauty. The *Aorere* passed close by; her deck and spars were of gleaming gold, her sails were cloth-of-gold; sparkles of light broke from the brass upon her wheel and the ripples at her foot; the unkempt, weather-beaten faces of her crew, turned sunward, were transfigured as if by triumph, and light flashed from heavy eyes.

By and by we rowed ashore in the whaleboat, and then I saw the *Tikirau*—she was the loveliest of them all! The naked, newborn radiance full upon her white hull, and broad upon the mainsail under which she was riding, there she swam upon the water like a shining sea-bird, with one gold-white wing uplifted, the quivering water-lights, blue and silver, playing upon her beautiful bows, and the gleaming glassiness below her faultless mirror. The white whaleboat, with her exquisite lines, was the worthy daughter of so beautiful a mother: I never could watch her leave the schooner's side without appreciating afresh that old imagination of the Maoris when first they saw the *pakeha* frigate with her pinnace—that the one was the parent-bird and the other the fledgling.

Three loads ashore, and then we were off again; and by noon were rounding a second great cape, East Cape, off which, at a little distance, lay a precipitous and barren islet, a mere, but mighty, rock. A zigzag path toiled up it, and on the top appeared the conspicuous white building of a lighthouse, with some lower roofs huddled beside. In our small vessel, and with the breeze then blowing, we were able easily to pass between the mainland and the rock, and, as we slid close by, 'Give 'em a good-day,' somebody suggested; 'it's a lonely life, that!' Every one of us, except the man at the wheel, accordingly seized something—anything that was handy, from one's neighbour's cap to the dinner-cloth—and waved it with hearty goodwill; and immediately, as if by magic, answering white signals broke from the watchful windows and doors above.

With the glass we could pick out the forms of women and little children; one mother had a baby in her arms. A lonely life indeed! and what a setting for the impressionable days of childhood—no trees, no grass, no birds except the sea-fowl, no paddock but the flat and barren tumble of sea, no room except for the eye, and, instead of the thousand-and-one friendly and pretty details of Mother Earth, simple, sheer, uncompanionable space. No bad abiding-place perhaps for a mind stored with theories calling for arrangement, or big with thoughts demanding birth—a kind of attic, indeed, of the Universe;

but what does a child make of it? and what does it make of the child? I should greatly like to know. The hardship of having to endure so anchored an existence seemed to us that day almost intolerable; for we ourselves were gloriously leaping and flying along before a gallant wind and over a sea of gleeful green and silver. There were islets of cloud in the sky, and these could travel with us; but that poor pinnacle of rock was swiftly left behind—left to rooted loneliness. Now it was a mere cloud on the horizon—now it was gone.

The port at which we called next had a pleasant distinction. It owned a bullock-cart. Generally speaking, upon that shallow and surf-beaten coast our men had to do a great deal of wading in the course of loading or unloading the whaleboat—weary work, with heavy kegs and cases on your back; so that it was a grateful relief at Waipiro to find a team of eight great bullocks, with a capacious cart attached, waiting in the surf for our boat-load. How picturesque they looked, too, in addition! with their wide-branched horns, and great bulks of glossy red and chestnut and black, very vivid above the vivid blue of the sea and whiteness of the surf, in the midst of which they stood patiently planted, like unusual rocks.

So the bright days ran on. Now we were at sea, now ashore; sometimes we hung off and on a little, to give the tide time to make or ebb, or the surf a chance to abate; once or twice, indeed, we were compelled to give up all hope of a landing, and to run past some expectant port or homestead; but, upon that lucky trip, not more than once or twice. Our return loads on the way down were mostly empty casks or cases ('Passenger with personal luggage,' I remember Mr Anstruther once unkindly announcing as they brought me back from shore upon a load of empty beer-barrels); but, as we proceeded south, we began, too, to take in some bales of wool. Would you care for a succinct and accurate account of a specimen day? Here it is, then, straight out of the ship's log, which was laboriously made up each night in the saloon by Mr Black (pipe in mouth, elbows spread, head laid upon one shoulder, severe frown on brow—can I not see him?), and which lies before me now as I write.

'*Tuesday*, 12/1/19—. At 5 a.m. lowered boat and landed cargo at 6.15 finished, started engine, secured boat and anchor went on to tuparoa and landed cargo, received 18 bales of wool on board at 10 a.m. finished and went on to reparoa and landed and shipped cargo at 2 p.m. set all sail secured boat and anchor and went on to port Awanui at 4 p.m. rounded E cape, light S. wind, 8 p.m. Howerea point abeam midnight calm clear weather. Barom 30, 20 pump and sidelights carefully attended to.

'John Black, Mate.'

The scenery changed as we proceeded south; not for the better from the picturesque point of view, though perhaps a farmer's eye might have found it more promising. The abrupt black crags and rocks of scoria gave place to the smooth smugness of *papa*, blank and biscuit-coloured; the proud, Bush-covered crests and deep gullies were supplanted by undulating grass-lands, treeless but for a spiky cabbage-tree here and there, a starry *ngaio* or so, and a good deal of *tauhinu* scrub, aromatic but unprofitable. A coach road, too, began to be visible, with now a trickling mob of sheep, now a vehicle or horseman proceeding along it. At Tolago Bay, Captain Fletcher showed me the place where Cook lay all one winter and overhauled his ship; as well as a strange, eerie spot in the hills nearby—a sort of deep grassy crater, at the bottom of which, through a great tunnel, the sea comes washing back and forth into the very heart of the hills.

And the scenery aboard the *Tikirau* changed too, as we neared our southernmost port of call. The 'farm-yard' boat had disappeared long before; its cabbages were now green but in memory, the cock, the cat, and the camellia had long been landed; day by day the casks diminished and the cases dwindled; day by day the leap into the whaleboat grew longer and the climb aboard more steep. There even came an hour when the final raft of timber went over the side; and at last, one fine morning, lo and behold! new-washed and immaculate, the actual planking of the deck appeared, and the vessel looked as strange as a familiar room does when all the furniture is out of it.

The next day we ran into Gisborne.

At Gisborne we lay some three or four days, discharging and reloading. Then, homeward-bound, and once more with a well-piled deck, the *Tikirau* went out again, to trade up the coast instead of down. Places, like people, are extremely different according to the way in which you approach them; and although we steered practically the same course, and called at pretty nearly all the same ports, our passage up, nevertheless, stands out clear in my memory as quite a different trip from our passage down. We had still, however, the same brilliant weather—I remember scarcely one grey day, although plenty of rough ones—it was still an epic of brightness, a long delightful tale of 'blue days at sea.'

Once we dipped our ensign, run up for the occasion, to a man-o'-war, whose trim hull and yellow funnels were dodging in and out among our remote haunts, taking soundings, we supposed; she looked like Behemoth in comparison with our insignificance. Once we sighted a whale, once we caught a young shark, and several times we had a porpoise hunt. These were quite exciting. One of the men, armed with a harpoon, would take his stand in the chains ready to strike at any polished back as it rose or rolled beneath him; another man stood by with a bowline to be slipped instantly over the tail of the 'catch' by way of support, while Floss and Darkie, rigid with excitement, paws upon the rail, hindfeet on the deck, rapturously barked and squealed. Once a porpoise did get 'fixed'; but the bowline was not ready at the moment, and the poor victim, breaking away from the harpoon, ripped a great square out of his back, and left a horrible stain upon the blue surface beneath which he shot away. 'Pity! His mates will eat him now, an' porpoise liver is as good as calf's any day,' said the regretful Nimrod in the chains. 'Ought to ha' looked a bit livelier with that there line, mate. But there! ought stands for "nothing," don't it?'

One beautiful evening we spoke another of our own fleet. We were anchored in a bay beneath mountains covered with Bush, which in one place was on fire, and sent a ruddy, pulsing glow across the sky and deep into the water. Opposite, in perfect contrast, hung the full moon, peaceful, and pure, and pale; and I was lying on the 'house' roof, lulled into delicious dreaminess by the humming of the surf ashore, the wash of the water along the vessel's side, and the satisfying loveliness all round, when—gradually—I became aware of an approaching, mystical presence; felt, rather than saw, a ghostly glimmer come gliding alongside; and there, by us, all of a sudden, in full moonlight, lay the white-winged *Rongomai*!

Her skipper came aboard the *Tikirau* and stood talking awhile on the deck; and something started him telling, in that tranquilly romantic place, a story of quite another side of the sea-life. It was a story that began with a wreck. The vessel had been thrown on her beam ends, the decks were a-wash, and the speaker, with only one other of the crew, found himself in the main-rigging, eye to eye with Death. 'The chap with me was a very smart young fellow—hard case, regular pirate, an', says he, "Watch below must ha' been drowned, an' the rest o' watch on deck looks to be well overboard. What say," says he, "if we was to try an' save her on our own, an' keep her for ourselves?" Well, she was under fore an' main torps'ls ('twas that what done it), an' first thing was, to get that main torps'l down. God! that was a business—aye, that *was* a bit of work! There she was, bangin' about, an' there was we, *bein'* banged—flesh and blood gettin' knocked clean out of us in lumps, though we knew nothin' about it till next day. Every minute, thinks I, "We'll never live to see another"; but hows'ever, down comes the blessed sail at last, an' then, what with the lift o' the sea, an' a lick o' wind that shifted her round, she started to right herself. An' now here comes in the cream o' the thing. We was beginnin' to move a bit smart about her, and heart'n' each other up, tellin' what a good deal we'd made of it, when, all of a sudden, blessed if a man's head don't pop up from below, with the rest of him followin'! an' then another, and another, an' another, with all the rest o' *them*—until there was *both our watches out on deck, and both full, mind you, not a hand missin'!* Bit of a sell, eh?—How's the wind? Southerly draw, ain't it?'

It must have been on the following night that we anchored opposite a great gully, or river-gorge, with a little native settlement at the mouth of it, and a small church, that, beside that great gash in the hills, and by the widespread sea, had somehow an air of facing all alone tremendous odds. The early mists were still upon the mountains, and the dew upon the seaside turf, when we landed our cargo next morning, and returned to the *Tikirau*. But we had barely got aboard before we noticed, streaming from the mouth of the gully, a long procession of people, some riding, others walking, and all advancing very slowly towards the church; and then the captain told us how he had heard ashore of the sudden death of a girl lately come out from England to keep house for her brothers away back there in the mountain Bush, and this was her funeral. We had finished our business at the place; and, as we bounded out again upon the brilliant sea, brightness, speed, and strength everywhere about us, light in our eyes, and full life racing through our veins, there was not one of us, I think, that was untouched. 'Travelling half the world over, eh?' as Tim put it, 'for *this*. Come all the way here, to find a grave.'

We re-entered Hicks Bay that same evening. No friendly riding-lights were this time to be seen; but, instead, there was a wonderful sunset. Great wafts and washes of pure fire suffused the sky, here and there narrowly separated by rifts of a clear blue-green, almost icily cold; and over all this bright delirium of colour, dark wisps and featherings of cloud seemed to have been wildly flung, and now to be lying in wait, as it were, with a sort of sinister stillness. 'A nice sunset, yes,' said the skipper; 'but, all I have against it, a windy one.' He was right, of course; and in Hicks Bay we lay, windbound, for the next five days.

What did we do all that time? Well, luckily for us, it was 'a dry blow,' and one from which the bay itself was well protected; so we went ashore and visited the natives, explored the rocks and beaches, and hunted about in the Bush for peacocks' feathers and late cherries. A shipwrecked crew had once 'dossed' for days in the bush, the men said, and we discovered their camp, and appropriated, for Tim's benefit, some of the lumps of coal still lying about. Then every day before dinner the men enjoyed what must have been truly a glorious sport. They would put on their oldest rig—I am afraid my presence aboard was a sad drawback here—dive from the bowsprit into the clear, dancing blue below, and there swim and tumble about, like so many dolphins, chasing each other round and under the vessel, and vigorously splashing the while to keep the sharks away. With what envy I watched them—I who could not swim! They used to try and persuade me to jump overboard and join them, promising not to let me drown, but I never had the nerve. I have been sorry for it ever since.

Then there was work to be done. The *Tikirau* had her hull painted during this enforced 'lay-up,' and went out of Hicks Bay looking more of a snowy sea-swallow than ever. And there was a settler to be 'removed' from his old house on one side of the bay to his new one on the other. We removed him; sitting patiently in the whaleboat while his beds and tables and chairs came casually down the breakneck track—some of them on a sledge, more of them off it—feasting upon apples from his orchard, which we roasted at a fire kindled on the rocks; and being feasted on in turns by multitudes of mosquitoes, who seemed to have been keeping Lent for years. It was the only place upon the coast where we met them, and the meeting was one they must have thoroughly enjoyed.

Phil, by the way, told a rather good mosquito yarn on this occasion. 'Two skippers,' he said, 'were having a kind of a talk about the mosquitoes they'd met. "Biggest ever I saw," says the one, "was when I was a-layin' once off the east coast of Africa. Whoppers they was—and *powerful*? why, look here, now, blest if a swarm of 'em didn't go bang through my mains'l one day, easy as stones through a parlour window. What d'ye say to that, now?" "Say?" says skipper number two. "Why, I should say as how they must ha' been the very swarm I met with once down Florida way. Whoppers as you state, and powerful, as you'd lead one to suppose; and every one o' them with his little legs rigged out in a pair o' canvas pants." '

Then, too, the men used to go off frequently upon fishing excursions. While we were at sea, lines baited only with native hooks of iridescent *pawa*-shell trailed often from the stern, and secured us a welcome change of diet; but while we were in the bay, fresh fish, dried and drying, hung daily in the shrouds, and Tim was relieved of some anxiety as to stores. Poor old Cookie! The delay was hard upon him. 'You know, I got word, last port, my little chap's worse,' he wailed, 'an' here we are stuck up in this hole of a hole, and maybe he's—'

'Now, never you fret, Tim,' interrupted kindly little Mr Black. 'Kids is no sooner down than they're hup. You look at my Ted, now. I was in just such another stew over him one trip—an' you know the kind of a young devil 'e is now. Sings like a bloomin' thrush, swears like a trooper, eats 'is five meals a day, and brings 'ome 'is money to 'is mother at the week-end reg'lar. You just take and cheer up, Timmie! It's on'y the little born angels wot 'oists their wings so quick; and I take it you and yours ain't fish and flesh, eh?' He backed out of the galley as he spoke, but he left Tim refreshed.

At last, too, we did get out of Hicks Bay, and round the Cape. After that a good deal of maize-shipping was done. Here and there, as we proceeded north, a smoke signal would go up ashore, the *Tikirau* would lie-to, and the whaleboat would fetch off the load. Sometimes the natives would come off in their own boats—I remember one that looked exactly like a flax-leaf, for it was painted bright green both inside and out, and had a gunwale of red—and our deck was full of brown faces and melodious with talk that lacked the 's'. The scene ashore meanwhile was most picturesque. Beside the open storehouses of bright yellow grain, groups of natives would be gathered about the fragrant fires of corn-cobs. Perhaps a few of the girls would be shelling maize, and a pretty sight that was. Dressed generally in dark-blue cotton, their long hair rippling glossy down their backs, they squatted beside the yellow heaps already shelled, against which their smiling faces showed like darkly sparkling jewels, and from between their brown fingers the maize fell fast from the cobs in showers of golden rain. The mothers, meanwhile, would most likely be using the signal-fire as a community cooking-stove. Roast sea-urchin I never could induce myself to taste, but steamed fish *à la Maori* is super-excellent, and never have I eaten more toothsome *kumaras* and potatoes than those taken all piping hot between the finger and thumb (one's own) and consumed without further sauce or ceremony, upon the windy beach.

Of my many hostesses, I remember especially one. She was very, very old—nearly a hundred years old, Phil maintained—and as she advanced to greet me I thought at first that never had I seen a wilder woman. Her face was one network of wrinkles; her hair, a remarkable reddish-brown in hue, was tied upon the top of her head in a fuzzy knot; her dress was an indescribable muddle of shawls, and perhaps her face might have been washed when she was fifty. Rich, yet scarce distinguishable at first, was the tattoo below her mouth; above it, at one corner, a cigarette stuck out. She made me heartily welcome, however, with outstretched hands full of baked *karaka* kernels, and a flood of talk and gestures. The talk, unhappily, I could not understand at all, and felt decidedly shy at first of the kernels; but the friendliness was irresistible: we squatted down side by side and entered into a brisk exchange of smiles.

Mr Anstruther meanwhile, Phil, and even Tom the diffident, kept shouting out to her something in Maori to which she made always the same reply, accompanied by many shakes of her dishevelled head and a certain air of dignified protectiveness that aroused my curiosity. When at last we had parted, with much cordiality and warm handshakes, and I had got back to the boat, I asked the men what they had been saying.

'Only wanted her to rub noses with you,' said they.

'Thank you,' said I, not, I fear, without a wriggle. 'And what did *she* say?'

'Said she wouldn't, 'cause she didn't believe you would like it.'

How glad I was that I had mastered my hesitation about those *karaka* kernels! 'Lady is as lady does'; and old Harete, the unkempt, the unwashed, has remained delightful to my memory ever since as one of the most perfect hostesses I ever met, one considerate before all things of the feelings of her guest. As for a Maori estimate of European gentlehood, did you ever hear this little story, which was repeated to me by the captain? Some up-country settlers were one day speculating as to the social status of a new arrival, who himself had fixed it so high that he could not possibly get down from it to help wash the dinner-dishes. There happened to be a Maori present, who solved the problem very simply. '*Rangatira* (real gentleman)? That fellow? No!' says this true Daniel come to judgment. '*Gentleman* gentleman never mind what work he do. *Piggy* gentleman very particular!'

Such were some of the incidents of our homeward trip. But it is with a voyage as it is with a life—you may chronicle every event, and yet leave out the essentials. The characteristic things are less the things that occasionally befall than those that continually *are*: and, as I look back, the main features and chief charms of that trip were just the common, everyday staples of it—the wholesome, hearty company aboard; the frankness and care-free-ness that come of living always with the open light, and air, and waters; and the inexhaustible riches of the eye. It was a life full of pictures. Day after day one woke to a different landscape (even when we were windbound, the ship's position altered, of course, with the tide), but never to one unenlivened by a foreground liquid and shining. Day by day, hour by hour almost, there was always a different sea. Now it would be rough and bright, then bright and smooth; now streeted with gold by the early sun, now one field of broad blue, or gallant blue-and-white; silver-and-green that flashed, or bloomy hyacinth, surely the true οἶνοψ—wine-dark. Sometimes it really looked asleep and dreaming, sometimes it glittered with argosies of sunbeams—or was it with 'innumerable laughter'? Now, it seemed sobbing and unquiet, as with grief; now it meant business, it was stern, fierce, even ferocious; now again it lay all molten silver, soft, tranquil, and at ease. Best of all, whatever its mood, it was always itself, always the living sea—restless, tireless, great: incomprehensible, yet the dear sister-soul of Man.

Then there was the excitement of landing through the surf—the waiting in smooth water between two huge white-crested breakers; the rowing back to meet the one astern, till it hung almost over us, and swamping seemed inevitable; the sharp swing skyward of the stern; the breathless, momentary poise and pause; then, the tremendous *thump* down, as the great wave passed beneath the boat; and, finally, our victorious rushing shoreward, upon its swift streams of snow. There were, too, the various, felt though unseen, glories of the air, that other wide ocean whose mercies were perpetually about us—its first freshness of a morning, its sweet intensity of cleanness when we were well out at sea, its evening aromas of sun-baked turf, warm *tauhinu*, and spicy smoke; and the splendour of its unreined vigour, when, rounding the sails like apples and piling the bright water into hills, it dashed us along through dashing music, and motion, and spray, and whipped one's blood to a wild, unreasoning exultation. Aye, one had three kingdoms in those days—the air, the sky, the sea; and a fourth, within; and all full to the brim with vigour.

And then there was the ship herself, real and companionable entity that she was: airy and beautiful creation somewhere between Nature and Man, and in touch with both; a marvel always, and always a friend. Seen from the shore, her white beauty drew the eye like a magnet, and gleamed like some jewel which the blue sea existed apparently only to set and so enhance; but the real heart of her beauty, as of all living things, lay in her *livingness*—and that, you must be aboard to feel. I used to love to get up in the bow, to watch her sharp white stem cleaving the wide water into twin curls of crystal, and taste the purity of the immense air as she divided it by her advance; then, turning, see her whole white, lovely self, coming as it seemed, towards me. Or, from the stern, to see her go about on a breezy day—deck all aslant, wind dinting the sails into deep hollows, sun filling them with gold, and pencilling them with the dun shadows of shrouds and dangling reef-points,water all a brave and white-capped boisterous blue on this side of her, roughly dark and silver on the other. And now it is 'Lee O!' from the captain, as he takes the helm, and the steersman runs forward to help in letting go the headsheets. Over goes the helm, out fades the wind from the great mainsail overhead, and like a disappointed, helpless thing, all the life out of it, there it hangs, listless, flat, unlit… till, as she recovers the breeze, first the headsails, then the fore, and finally the mainsail fill and swell out again; again all is taut above, a great, plump cheek of gold, and away and away we dance, all alive, over the buoyant water, and through the singing air. Or perhaps the boom is being gybed, and swings deliberately over above our heads, to the strain of brawny shoulders at the bitts, and a hoarse accompaniment of 'Come in! Way-hay! Ay-way! Hay-ho! As she will! Now then! Again! As she must! Come in!' Or we are just coming to anchor and it is, 'Haul down your outer jib!' in stentorian tones from the wheel. 'Haul down outer jib,' in obedient response from the bow… more orders, further echoes. Then the rattling of the anchor-chain over the deck, the scamper of the hands to make down fore and main sail and, lo! the *Tikirau*, with her wings furled—and yet how beautiful still!—and tethered, and yet how still alive!

Often when evening came and the rest of our mates that were not on duty had turned in, the dogs and I would get up on the house roof, and there, warm between their slumbering forms, I might watch the night come on. First, the late grave twilight, sky and water both fading, stars peeping out dim-eyed above the swinging trucks; then, glimmering dusk, with points of light brightening out all around, and faint wakes beginning to trail down through the guessed-at glassy swell; last, the immense Dark, powdered with sparkling constellations overhead, infinite in number, each one a world; and paved with a floor of wandering blackness, here and there streamered with light from above, and with a pathway of softest wool-white glimmering astern, jewelled by the phosphorus with green-twinkling beads and balls. And all the while, and all around, silence—perfected as it seemed, rather than broken, by the faint, pleasantly familiar ship-sounds—the movements of the wheel, the quiet creak of block and tackle, the whisper of the wind, and tapping of reef-points on the sail, the talking of the water to the side. And through the silence and the darkness the vessel, above all: the vessel, gently curtseying on her way, seeming almost to breathe beneath one as she rose and fell with the heaving of the sea-breast; such a speck in the universe, all alone, and yet so sure; a creature not seaworthy alone, but world-worthy.

But why multiply words? No summary of their details could ever give the living spirit of those sea-days, no description ever convey their incommunicable charm. The voyage finished as it had begun— emphatically, with a couple of days' grand gale. But this time the wind was in our favour, and we flew before it. How it rained! how it roared! The mainboom, usually so serenely high overhead, was now continually sousing in and out of the wild water; the sail scooped up sea, tons of it, as well as wind; a double reef had shortly to be taken in it—and with what envy and admiration I watched my mates accomplishing the task! barefoot along the plunging boom, torn at by the wind, swamped by the sea, knocked and beaten by the canvas, but all the while, active as cats and resolute as men, steadily getting the points tied, as a matter of course.

Our last sunrise saw the Auckland windows flash. We had been away just a month. As we sailed up the harbour, 'My old hen can see me now,' said Mr Black, in the tones, if not perhaps the usual terms, of sincere affection.

'See that sheet waving out at that window there?' said Mr Anstruther. 'My mother never misses our coming in.'

'Steak and eggs for tea to-night, Tim,' stipulated Phil.

'Steak an' eggs! Vot nonsense is zat?' growled Fritz. 'Zozzages… big!' And Tim beamed upon them both, for he had had news at the port before that his little sick son was better. It was only the passenger who made a little private moan to herself, as we made fast to the wharf, and the jolliest holiday she had ever had in her life was over. She was but little consoled, although certainly much cheered for the moment, by the discovery among her possessions, that first night ashore, of a damp parcel insinuated somehow among them, and labelled, 'A keepsake from the *Tikirau*,' in Mr Anstruther's hand.

It contained a large slab of duff.

Alas, the *Tikirau*, beautiful and beloved! Facing so willingly all the chances of the sea, she was not spared their last extreme of tragedy. A little while ago, from the deck of a bigger but not a better vessel, bound on the same trip, Captain Fletcher pointed out to me, upon the beach near one of the little ports we had touched at that bright summer, a white, lopsided object. It looked like the hull of a boat, or part of it, turned upside down. 'There,' said he, 'that's all that's left of the *Tikirau*,' and neither of us said much more. Carrying, as at least I might be thankful to learn, none of her old crew, she had been caught at a dangorous anchorage, one winter's night, by a terrible, suddenly-veering storm, and perished with every soul on board. No light without shade, it seems, even in a ship's career. So ended, in gloom, that busy, bright, seeming-sentient existence.

But I never think of it as ended at all; in my private and particular cosmos, the world of my experience, safe for me still sails the *Tikirau*! Staunch, willing, and nimble, a friendly and a happy ship, there for ever she hastens upon her sparkling way, a winged and snow-white presence, bright as a sea-bird in the sunshine, or a flake of flying foam: still linking little green port with little green port along the flashing blue: still beautifying the seas, still gilding humdrum matters with romance: livening duty with beauty, buoyantly taking risks, bright, beneficent, and brave.

# Café au Lait

The long, curving main street of the little harbour town looked very bright and clean. Half the houses seemed to have been just freshly painted; some were yellow, some white, and most of the roofs were red. There had been a little spring shower, too, and now the wet asphalt of the side-walk shone nearly as blue as the bright, new-washen sky, and the heart-shaped lilac-leaves in the little garden beside the shop were tossing in soft, moist airs, and glittering with wetness and light. One branch was in flower already, and its plumes of dark, chocolate buds, and blossoms of fresh, pale purple looked almost audaciously young. The old bush that bore it came of stock that had crossed the ocean more than half a century before; but what did this little bough care about that? its blossoms were new this year. As the wind swung it, now it sprang jauntily up towards the sky, now it swept down towards the springing green grass, and now it scattered a whole shower of sparkling rain-diamonds over the crown of Philippe's rusty black hat, as he passed beneath the lilac-bush and out into the road.

The wife of the man to whom he had last year sold the shop, and with whom he now boarded, was standing at the open door beside the windowful of clocks. 'Why, Mr Philip!' she said, in a tone of diffident remonstrance, 'ain't it almost a bit too damp for you to get your walk to-day?' But old Philippe merely raised his hat, and stalked on past her. He did not like to be interfered with by people who had not the right—and who had? Mrs Watchmaker Brown, for her part, looked after him with a mixture of feelings, as he took his way, rather waveringly, up the street. She was a kindly-hearted woman, but he was a 'proud,' unsociable old man. He did look really very feeble. She could hardly help thinking that, if 'anything should happen'…

why, after all, it would be nice to have the whole house to themselves.

Poor 'proud' Philippe! The air, as it blew in, sweet and fresh from the sea, gathered more sweetness yet from the blossomed gardens that divided the painted houses; Mrs Selincourt's wallflowers breathed so strong that even he could smell them; the sunshine soothed with a delicious warmth his withered, sunken cheek—it was spring, yes: but Philippe did not look much like spring. His bent and lean old figure, his cadaverous, pale face, spoke far more plainly of the end of things than of any fresh beginning. All the winter through, old Philippe had been ill. It was only within the last few days that he had been able to put on his queer 'outlandish' shoes and get outside at all; and that famous cherry-wood stick of his, with the curling handle and the *edelweiss*-flower carved on it, really needed now to be what Bossu had in jest been wont to call it—'The old man's third leg.'

Ah, Bossu... so *he* was gone!... buried a month ago, they said. Old Bossu, last but one of all those thirty-five shipmates who had come out to Pakarae from Havre upon *La Belle Etoile*, fifty-one years ago. Fifty-one years is a long time. They had built, those early settlers, that curving street of quaint, two-storeyed, gabled houses so much prettier than New Zealand houses are wont to be; they had planted the walnut-trees and willows, the peaches and poplars and the vines: they had bequeathed to this little, out-of-the-way angle of British territory its subtle, still persistent 'foreign' flavour; and now they were all living, all, all but one, very far away from Provence and Savoy, with white stones at their heads, in the little cemetery yonder, underneath the sighing pines.

Certainly they had left children; the old names were still to be seen upon the corners of the streets, and above shop-doors. But they were barbarously mispronounced, these names; and, as for the children, who had grown up in this, the country of their birth, they were all British now—there was to be found among them scarcely one who could make shift to stammer, and that with an accent truly frightful, three syllables of his father's tongue. For the last five years, Philippe and Bossu had been the last remaining representatives of '*la patrie*,' the sole survivors of the 'Originals'... And Bossu now was gone!

Yes, he was gone! Here, halfway up the street, was his house, all shut up. The green shutters—Bossu's was the only house that had retained the gay green shutters of Home—were fast closed; springing grasses, and darkly shining wreaths of periwinkles, lit with purple stars, hid kindly the unwashen step, and surged against the never-opening door. Upon the little lawn, smooth once as Bossu's hairless head, the scythe was now sadly needed, and shears should long since have been used about the shell-paved weeping-ash arbour where the two old comrades had been wont to sit together, to smoke their pipes of modern (how inferior!) tobacco, to drink the Australian vintage that compared, how unfavourably! with the old, rough red *vin du pays*, and to speak one with another the dear old tongue. Bossu, it is true, had been of France, not of Switzerland, and had been wont, therefore, at times, to suggest alternatives to Philippe's phrases and pronunciation; not always without a little natural irritation on both sides; Ninon had often had to allay excitement. Still he had been, in some sort after all, a compatriot, and in all ways a comrade.

And Ninon, too. Not so pretty, not so pretty, as that earlier, fresher Ninon, laid to rest—could it be, *eh, mon Dieu!* forty-two years since? in the little churchyard *over there* by the milk-white glacier-stream... but named for her, and young like her, and kind—Ninon, too, was gone away; they said, to the married sister in the North Island: there was nobody left! And a shingle, see! was off the roof; the chimney needed repairing, the gate swung loose. The old place was staunch enough to last for years to come, if it were but properly looked after, but, left all to itself like this, it would soon grow damp, it would quickly rot, and young Bossu would presently have excuse enough to pull it down and build upon its site that cheese-factory he was for ever speaking of. Milk and money, milk and money—that was all this country ever cared about... And the old house did remind one so of Home!

Ah-h-ha! What was this—this delicious, this reviving whiff of some perfume truly familiar! Coffee! Yes, coffee—in berries—being roasted. But who, then, actually roasted coffee still, in these lax days? Ah, Métrailleur, to be sure—Métrailleur *fils*, who kept the grocery store past which the old man's feet were just now languidly bearing him: Joseph Métrailleur, who called himself nowadays Meat-railer, if you please! in deference, forsooth, to the British tongues of his customers. Yes, Joseph was roasting coffee beans—and when he had roasted them and ground them up, and tempered the flavour a little—oh, judiciously, without doubt, for Joseph was a worthy man—he would put the mixture into some tin whose lid was loose, or lost, perhaps; and in the course of the next six or seven months would sell it, doing it up in paper bags, to people who would make it as they did tea and then offer it one to drink. Did not he, Philippe, know? Sore had been his longing for some coffee during his tedious convalescence; and once, in response to his repeated requests and as a great treat for the poor old foreigner, Mrs Brown, the well-meaning, the incapable, had served him, with noisy anticipations, a muddy *tisane* which it would have disgraced a pig to drink. But this, which Métrailleur had not yet gone beyond roasting—ah, this was coffee indeed! and Philippe halted his steps, and stood still for quite a little while outside the grocery door, drinking in, with his heart even more than his sense, that exquisite aroma—subtle, magical. Melmotte's tame penguin, with its broken leg, its yellow eyes, that seldom spied a live fish nowadays, and useless flippers that never felt the waves, came waddling up to greet a fellow-exile, and assumed a portly, sprawling attitude almost upon Philippe's feet. But the old man never noticed him—how should he? He was sixty years, and half the world, away.

... Outside, all was shining. The early sunshine was bringing out every rich tone of brown and red in the resinous timbers of the old chalet. Inside, the coffee-berries were roasting, roasting. Ah, the good smell! Ah, the first morning freshness! Now he himself, Philippe, *le petit Philippe*, in his clean blue blouse and wooden shoes, stood dutifully crushing the brown berries in the coffee-mill fastened to the table... now, again, his mother bent above him with a shining-bright, long-spouted pot in either dexterous hand, from which the good streams of boiling milk, and real black coffee, velvety yet clear, descended to a perfect union within the handless bowl of green earthenware. And, all the while, the cuckoo calling and calling outside, and the rocky rivulet running down the mountain, merrily, even as he himself would presently run merrily down to school. Ah, the good mother, the old home, the long, long ago! Jumbo, the penguin, tired of inattention, here pecked viciously at Philippe's foot, and the old man moved absently on up the street.

Here was the Pakarae church-belfry: differently roofed with those red tiles, it was true, and rather squat than lofty, yet in its shape, a bell-hat on top of a tower, how curiously like the one at St Armand! Upon the mountains on the other side the harbour there was still some snow—stainless as the snows of old, above Barue: and the harbour itself, so shut in by these spring-green paddocks, so satin-smooth to-day, did not look any more like the salt and separating sea, it looked precisely like the little lake of Mec; the jetty, too, though he had never noticed it before, was the wooden twin of that one to which old Mathieu's boat had been wont to bring an occasional tourist in search of his father's beautiful wood-carvings, his *boiserie*…

… What were these globe-like yellow flowers in old Mrs Pochette's garden? She had never had them before; or at least he had never re-marked them before. Surely, surely—they were that very same yellow ranunculus of which he had been used to pluck bouquets for Ninon in that lush riverside pasture by old Fleury's mill! *Boules de beurre*, she called them, or sometimes *boules d'or*—butter-balls, or balls of gold. He remembered! Only those flowers of Home were finer—every-thing at Home was finer. Why should he think so much of Home this morning? Hark! wasn't that surely the cuckoo now? Alas, no; only a sea-bird, and how tired he felt all of a sudden! *Miséricorde*, how tired! Yonder to the right, only a very little way up the hill, was that sunny paddock of Métrailleur's that had the dry rocks in it. He would go and sit a little on those rocks and rest. Why not?… There, at last! How very fatigued he was! Ah, how weary!

Métrailleur's paddock was a long, grassy slope, with a fine view

out over the lake above the clustered roofs of Pakarae. Just now, in all
the glory of its spring verdure, it looked like a stripe of the freshest
and softest green velvet, only here and there the exquisite surface was
roughened by a little outcrop of grey, volcanic rock. A little below one
such lichened ledge, on which Philippe had seated himself, there ran
a belt of pine-trees; a snow peak soared above them in the distance
across the harbour; and, beyond their spiry tips and between their
latticed boughs, the lake spread out its blue, bloomy sheen, full of
violet and green hill-mirrorings. There were cows in the paddock;
cows with richly shining skins, of fawn and white and chestnut; and
one of them, a velvety black creature, wore a bell about her neck, that
tinkled musically as she browsed. The little bright, brown creek, on
its headlong way through the paddock from the summits above to
the sea beneath, tinkled also, and sprang from rock to rock with a
shining and merry delight. And the sun was cloudless, the bright air
was thin, and crisp, and pure; there was an Alpine look and feeling
everywhere—it all was really very like Switzerland. Philippe, as he sat
there resting in the sun, began mistily to wonder which of the spring
Alp-flowers were out yet, and actually looked about him for some,
in the fresh, green grass. For the little thin white crocus that follows
the heel of the melting snows it was of course too late, and for the
fairy fringe of the violet soldanella; but a cowslip or two, surely? some
gay little bright pink primula, or sulphur-coloured anemone? above
all, at least one gentian, one bright little star of heaven's own blue, to
look up at one with the face of a friend upon this sunny, green Alp?

There was, of course, not one. Moreover, the little hut beside the
pines, as Philippe's fixed gaze at last slowly apprehended it, revealed
itself most plainly to be wrought of no dear picturesque dark timbers,
but of galvanised iron only, pale and ugly. The old man roused himself
out of his waking dream. He sighed. Ah, yes! it might certainly all
be very like, but it was not the same—it was not Home! There are
times when similarities do but accentuate a difference; and a wave
of the most bitter yearning and homesickness overwhelmed poor
Philippe now as he sat there in the sun.

O for the Real Things—for the lake that was not salt, for the streamlet that flowed from snows, for the grass all full of flowers! O for the old Home landscape, for the old, familiar speech, for the dear, the true, the real, the right, old ways! Philippe had not been in Switzerland for half a century; his youthful manhood, his prime, his age, had all been passed in New Zealand; and he was in general extremely proud of his adopted country, of her beauty, her resources, her rapid growth, her happy and spring-like prospects. But now, on this radiant morning, whether it was the result of his years, of his illness, or of some rare climatic quality of the day, it seemed to him that he had made a great mistake, that he had been somehow duped, defrauded, ruined; that he had been made to spend all his strength, all his life, in the wrong place. And for the right one, for that far-away lost country, of his childhood, of his early strength, of his first and only love, a desperate longing fed by all these strangely reawakened memories and associations grew and grew, until it overwhelmed him: until there was no more room in his mind for anything but remembrance, no more room in his heart for anything but regret. It was the true, the terrible nostalgia. He wanted his country, his own familiar country, as a little child wants its mother, as a sick child cannot do without her; and the slow, pathetic, helpless tears of old age escaped from his closed eyes, and ran down his pallid cheeks unhindered.

So possessed was he by the agony of this strong yet impotent yearning that he never noticed certain shuffling footsteps which now came near to him, and halted, and then again shuffled hesitatingly away. Presently, however, they returned.

'Mister finds himself not well?' a voice said softly. Philippe opened his eyes with a start.

An old woman was standing before him. She had on a brown stuff dress, bulkily gathered in at the waist, and a large apron of very dark blue linen; on her head, instead of a hat, there was a three-cornered yellow checked handkerchief; and under one arm she carried a round wooden milking-stool, in the other hand a bucket of milk. Just so, exactly, Philippe remembered his own mother to have looked, on any midday of her life; and he looked at the vision in bewilderment. Yet this woman was not his mother—she had not his mother's face. Her own, however, was full of so mother-like a compassion and sympathy that it spoke straight to his heart, and drew an answer from it.

'I have been ill,' he faltered, as naturally and as appealingly as a child; and then he felt ashamed, and turned away his head. He did not know how far that child-like impulse had decoyed him, or that he had spoken those words not only in the tone but in the speech in which he would have said them to his mother. But his hearer did, for it was the patois of her own native *canton* that she had heard.

'*Eh, mon Dieu!*' she ejaculated; '*mon Dieu!*' She set down, first, her bucket of milk and her stool with all the carefulness of the good housewife; and then she clasped her hands, looked up with streaming eyes to heaven, and addressed, surely to every saint in the calendar, a medley of thanks and lamentations and thanks again, of which Philippe understood every word, for it, too, was in his native tongue.

' You are of Mec, *ma mère*, of Boissy?' he inquired with eagerness, when at length she paused for breath.

'I am of Evremond, monsieur,' she replied. Philippe grew very white. It had been the village next his own.

' Ah, you know then the bridge,' he said hoarsely. 'You know the church of St Armand? And the house of Martin the miller, that stands midway between the church and the bridge?' He could scarcely breathe as he finished.

'But which bridge?' inquired the old woman. 'And which church would monsieur distinguish, since there now are several? But as for the house of Père Martin, the miller—ah, yes—but it is twenty years since that was pulled down. There stands a fine, magnificent hotel in its place now,' she added with pride, 'and the railway runs by the stream.'

'How! Through Fleury's pasture?' cried Philippe in dismay.

'Fleury's pasture? I know it not. But yes, it is of course that, that, in these days, is the station,' she replied. 'One sees well that monsieur certainly cannot have been at St Armand within these great many years. Oho, the little place! it has grown all out of the memory of that which it used to be, as a little child grows out of his shift. Many people come now to St Armand year by year. The steamboat brings them twice in the day, and, of a summer evening, the band plays on the fine pier where once was the old black jetty; and the pleasure-parties dance.'

' And the churchyard?' Philippe stammered out. He was growing paler and paler.

'The churchyard? Oh, the churchyard of the old, the little, church—that, yes, assuredly that remains,' she answered soothingly, with quick, instinctive comprehension.

Apparently, however, it was almost all that did remain of Philippe's own old St Armand. To every one of his succeeding questions her answers came ever the same. 'Gone, changed, this or that instead.' The little secluded hamlet had in fact been 'discovered' by tourists and hotel-proprietors; and Philippe as he listened perceived, with a horrible sinking of the heart, that, could he at that moment have been miraculously restored to his native place, he would have found it unrecognisable. Home? Home was gone; it no more existed; it was no longer real. There was no such place in the world any more! A dizziness came over him.

'Monsieur must please to drink!' said the old woman's voice in his ear, with a note of authority. She was supporting his head, Philippe suddenly found, and holding to his lips a wooden bowl, the like of which he had not seen for fifty years. Somehow, he did not seem to mind this woman's ministrations—they were not at all like poor Mrs Brown's—and he obeyed her without irritation, and swallowed the draught of warm milk. It revived him.

'A bowl of coffee would have been better,' he heard her mutter as though to herself, and was able actually to smile.

'Seat yourself, *ma mère*,' he presently directed in his turn. 'And tell me how it comes that you too are at Pakarae.'

It was very simple. The old woman, it appeared, was Joseph

Métrailleur's grandmother. Her husband had died, over there at Evremond, some months before, and she had found herself without kith or kin or any one to look after ('I, who am still so very strong, monsieur,' she said, in a tone of expostulation), excepting these unseen, far-away relations in New Zealand. After them, since she was one of those to whom all kin seem kind, her heart had longed; to them surely she might be of use in the new, rough country? So she had written to them, begging piteously that she might come out, and Joseph's good, impulsive heart had been touched; he had assented, he had helped, she had arrived at Pakarae during the winter, while Philippe had been ill—and now here she was, poor soul! forbidden by both pride and sense of fairness, to beg for repatriation ('Only figure to yourself, monsieur, the expense! and whom, in addition, have I, there?'), and yet a most bewildered stranger in a most strange land, unbelievably homesick and lonelier, alas! than ever. For Joseph, yes, he was indeed a good one, he, a perfect heart of gold, but ever at the shop: Suzanne the wife, she too, oh certainly, was also good, but… as was no more than natural, she had her own ways, she did not understand the old woman's, she did not require her help: while as for the child, the little Suzee—the old dame stopped abruptly.

'And you?' asked Philippe. 'What is your name?'

It, was, if monsieur pleased, she answered meekly, 'Nanette.' Nanette! It sounded so like Ninon that Philippe's face grew white again. Nanette was much concerned.

'It is very easy to see,' she observed, 'that monsieur has indeed been ill. Monsieur requires attention, above all, he should have nourishing food. A good soup, now, with cabbage in it, a cutlet, a tender *poulet* with salad, a flask of white wine, and a good little cup of coffee to bury it all—black, with cognac.'

Philippe felt his long-lost appetite come suddenly back as she enumerated with zest the savoury details of this once-familiar menu. It was with a heart-felt sigh that he answered, perhaps a little impatiently:

'Yes, yes! But then it is impossible to get such things here—the right things—properly prepared——'

'Why not? I will wager that I can prepare them,' interrupted Nanette with a confident chuckle—which ended in the middle, however, and her good old face clouded over. 'It is true!' she said, in her turn with a sigh. 'I have not my own kitchen, my own utensils. Here, one puts the potatoes into the water, the *gigot* into the oven, by and by one makes the mouth-wrying tea, the *tisane* that so ravages the interior—and the dinner is served. One eats, one is fed, it is true; but that is not to say one has dined. The very stomach is an exile in this land.'

And Philippe sadly assented. He knew so well that dinner, even now awaiting him at Mrs Brown's. A thousand times already he had eaten of it, and the thousand and first made no appeal to him. Most of all did his languid appetite resent the suggestion of that 'long-stood' cup of tea. Tea, indeed! Again he seemed to smell the aroma of that coffee, freshly roasting at the store; and again it spoke to him of comforts, not so much of the body as of the mind, the heart.

They talked on and on, still in the old pleasant dialect. Nanette was younger than Philippe; she had married early in life, and so had her son, the father of Joseph; still, she was able to tell her countryman the fortunes of nearly all the old friends he so eagerly inquired after, and, alas, alas! those fortunes, as it seemed, with scarcely one exception, were all finished! Philippe felt his heart, his horizon, painfully contract. Each death, as Nanette recorded it in her simple chronicle, sounded to him like yet another stroke of the tolling bell at the burial of all that had once made Home. He sighed again and again as she proceeded. What was there left? And yet, for all the sadness, what a sweetness, too, in hearing again those well-loved names, in speaking the remembered childhood tongue, in being understood!

'Gran'ma! gran'ma!' called suddenly a very shrill and consequential little voice; and in at the paddock-gate next minute there ran a very emphatic little girl. With her starchy pinafore-frills, her perked-up hair-ribbon, her lifted eyebrows and sharp little nose, she somehow presented the effect of having been sharpened into a point all over.

'Why, here you are, all the time! an' I've been hunting an' hunting for you, gran'ma,' she proclaimed indignantly. 'You're just to come right straight home this very minnut—mumma says so. Here's mumma coming now, her own self,' she ended, with a pout; and in fact a very stout woman, with a large, florid, good-natured, but rather stupid face, was to be seen just entering the paddock-gate. She puffed and panted as she came.

'Why, gran'ma,' she called out wheezily, 'I'm sure I'm right-down glad to see you safe. We just couldn't make out what was keepin' you—thought old Blackberry must ha' knocked you over or something. Joe, he's a-give her that black cow, an' she will milk her midday, as well as mornin' an' evenin'—an' it *does* keep the dinner about so,' added Mrs Métrailleur, between gasps, and rather apologetically, to Philippe, of whom, like almost everybody else in Pakarae, including even the acute little Susy, she stood somewhat in awe.

'It is the custom, where she comes from,' Philippe answered stiffly. He did not like to see the bewildered, helpless expression now stultifying Nanette's kindly face; she looked nearly as dull as Mrs Métrailleur herself. 'We are of the same country, Madame and I,' he added, with a courteous bow in her direction.

'Why now, just think o' that!' responded the worthy Mrs Métrailleur, mildly interested. 'It's a pity you don't want no housekeeper, Mr Philippe—not but what I know Mrs Brown does for you, an' she's as good as the next two, as they say. On'y you'd understand the old lady's ways, an' her lingo, an' they're both beyond me, I'm sure. Been sick quite a long time, ain't you? you must mind an' take good care o' yourself now—look as if you could do with a real good old feedin' up, so you do—an' that reminds me, gran'ma, your dinner will be all dried; I put it in the oven; Susy an' I done ours. You won't come in an' have a bite with her, Mr Philippe, I s'pose? I'd make you a real good cup o' tea… Well, you must drop in some other time, then, an' have a chat with gran'ma. We'd be pleased to see you any time, I'm sure. Joseph, he was sayin' on'y at breakfast what a lot he thought o' you. Come on, gran'ma. Bless you, she don't take in more than half a word at a time o' what I say! Goodbye, Mr Philippe.'

'Come on, gran'ma!' repeated Susy, officiously. 'An' why ever in the world didn't you go an' put a hat on, instead of that silly old hankey?' she added loudly as they went away—resolved that Mr Philippe should see there was one member of the family knew what was proper, anyhow. Susy was universally reckoned 'a pretty smart little girl.'

Philippe watched the three of them thoughtfully, as they crossed the paddock and entered Métrailleur's back-door; he sat thinking for a minute or two longer, and then he too left the velvety paddock, and went back down the street. Like the poor old Nanette, he also was late for dinner; and Mrs Brown, although she would not dare to scold, he knew would have upon her face that aggrieved, martyr-like expression that he found always so peculiarly irritating. As for the dinner, the dinner could go to the dog—the only creature it was fit for... That coffee still smelt very good as he passed the store. What if he stopped and bought some? A little of it for breakfast, now, mixed with plenty of good milk—the milk of this country was all right, if it could be flavoured with coffee. Ah, but then, the coffee must be made, not murdered! It was no use buying any to take home to Mrs Brown.

There were two men busy by the fence of old Bossu's house as he came past. They were putting up a sign—'To Let,' it said, quite plainly. Young Bossu did not mean to pull the old place down just yet, then—Ah!... Philippe stood suddenly stock-still, staring at the green shutters but not seeing them at all, in the full radiance of the idea that, ever since Mrs Métrailleur's remarks, had been slowly dawning on his mind. He, Philippe, was not poor; the old house was not large; Bossu *fils* could not demand an extortionate rent, and, in the little paddock at the back, Nanette could keep her cow. Such were the simple, practical thoughts that were at work, altering his whole world for him. The old woman, the old house, the old man—why not convert them all, by associating them in one companionship, into a little remnant of departed Home?

No rash idea of marriage was in old Philippe's mind. Nanette, the withered everyday housewife, could never be a rival to Ninon, the ideal, the ever-young—neither would she, in her peasant meekness, ever dream of such a thing. But she could be his housekeeper, his *bonne*; they could have again, between them, the old tongue, the old ways, the memories of old. She would not have to put up any longer with Mrs Métrailleur and the terrible Susy; he could escape from Mrs Brown. Nanette could make him omelettes, like his mother's; he could eat them out of doors, within the leafy ash-tree arbour, as they used to eat at Home. Ah, Home! Home was gone, vanished, dead—surviving only in his brain—and in hers... Well, one must just make the best of where one was; there would be something to make the best of, now. Why, she could make him coffee! Swiss coffee to mingle with New Zealand milk. Eh, and what if, at the same time, one could mingle with the insipidity of the present something of the poetry, the aroma, of the beloved past?

*Café au lait*, properly prepared, is delicious.

Poor Mrs Brown, watching with long-suffering Philippe's tardy progress down the street, had presently the additional annoyance of seeing him, when he had at last got within two yards of her gate, suddenly cross the road, and walk into young Bossu's, with a step grown wonderfully firm.

# The Old Kitchen

Out towards the tip of a certain bare, seaward-stretching promontory, there stands a thick, dark tuft of pines, and within the pines an old farm, painted white. Years and years ago, when Kiteroa, the scattered settlement inland, was still green virgin Bush, a young man planted the pines, which a very little child could then have jumped over, set up a *whare* in their midst, and brought home his bride. The wind blew furiously across those open slopes upon the adventurous plantation, the driven rains beat on and through the *whare* weather-boards, as yet so unprotected. But the young couple fetched up clay from the creekside and built double walls to their home, with a solid lining of earth between; while for their precious trees they reared a stout bulwark of planks. The planks have decayed long since, and the *whare* has given place to a large old rambling house, which, deep within its tall and spicy green breakwind, can sleep in peace now through the wildest weather. One of its rooms, however, is still warm with earth-lined walls, and looks out far to sea.

The young couple throve and prospered. Children were born in the single room of the little low dwelling; played about between its walls of bare brown wood; were warmed and fed by its great, open hearth with the Colonial oven, that took up nearly all one side of the place; and peeped through its one window at the great spread of sea down there beyond the garden, and at the snow-peaks over the sea. The brood all flourished; and by and by had grown so much, both in size and numbers, that the roof which sheltered them must needs grow too; the *whare* had now to delegate some of its functions, part with some of its importance, and, instead of providing a whole home by itself, become one room, merely, among others.

But it was still the chief room, kitchen, dining-room, parlour, and family living-room. Within this little square of space that had so faithfully nursed their infant spring and outgush, the flowing, growing currents of affairs circled more vigorously than ever; until at last they overflowed it. A new kitchen was then built at the other end of the house, and the old one, separated from it by a whole chain of bedrooms, became a sitting-room. Nobody in that house, however, had much leisure to sit; and the stream of activity, though running now more briskly than ever, was quite diverted in its course from the old kitchen, and visited it only at rare intervals, and then but meagrely. The old room, often for weeks together, was left to its silent survey of sea and garden, and its memories of past days.

By and by, as the years went on, the young couple grew old, and the children grew up, and, one by one, grew out of the old home, for all its additions. Then the father and mother died; and one of the daughters, already a middle-aged woman, came to live at the farm with her husband. But she had no children, and did not use half the house. A room more conveniently close to the modern kitchen was made into her sitting-room, and the old kitchen, at the other end of the house, was shut up. It was as if Life had now quite done with it.

The farm, high as it stands, and bare to the air and light—for the sea stretches wide below it upon three sides, and from it you can see the sun rise out of the water of a morning, and all but sink in it at night—dwells yet in a kind of retirement of its own. There is no made road leading to it, for one thing—only a rough track across the tussock and nodding blue-bells of the cliff; and the configuration of the slope on which it stands, swelling suddenly out into a crest of grey rock on the inland side, hides it from the coach-road, and has really the effect, in fact, as well as in appearance, of separating it from the rest of the settlement. The itinerant drapers and clockmenders, the book-agents and tea-travellers, even the old Syrian pedlar, with his trays of glittering gewgaws, were all apt to leave it unvisited on their rounds. Neighbours found it more natural to invite and welcome Mrs Callender to their own homes than to set out towards hers, there upon the road to nowhere.

It was with the more surprise, therefore, that Mrs Callender, one
wet June morning, found herself confronted on her doorstep, among
the winter violets, by a stranger, a lady; come, of all extraordinary
errands, to inquire whether Mrs Callender would not take her in to
board! She was all alone, and wished for a quiet lodging. It was her
intention to give music-lessons in the district.

Music! It is doubtful whether any other key would at that time
have opened Mrs Callender's independent door to a boarder; but
that one did, and instantaneously. The stranger, a tall, gaunt, short-
spoken woman, with hair already grey, and a stern, sad face, did not
look as though she would prove, or would even attempt to prove, an
otherwise congenial companion, but—if she played! If she would only
play! Mrs Callender had a passion for music, quite untrained, but
genuine and deep; melody was as thoroughly a need of her nature
as warmth was, or food, or air, and it was one that, away back here
in the country, she had never been able to appease. So she came to
terms at once; there was some throwing open of long-closed windows
and doors, a little sweeping and dusting, rubbing and rearranging;
and presently, a day or two after, the bullock-sledge came lumbering
over the tussock with a few battered boxes and one great wooden
case; and the old kitchen, with its brown walls, its great hearth, and
its outlook on the far horizon, passed into the possession of Miss
Kirkcaldie and her piano.

Who Miss Kirkcaldie was; where she had come from, and why;
how she had happened to drift into this out-of-the-way corner of
the world—these were questions that every one in Kiteroa asked,
but nobody could answer. Miss Kirkcaldie herself was Scotch, so
much was easily certain; and, being Scotch, she knew how to hold
her tongue; in fact, she might be said never to let go of it. She possessed, in addition, the much rarer power of disposing other people
to hold theirs, at least while in her company; in general she was
chilly, dignified, austere, and, upon occasion, had no difficulty in
being deaf as well as dumb.

But she was 'no trouble' to Mrs Callender; her modest dues were discharged with the utmost punctuality; and, whatever uncertainty might otherwise hang mistily about her, her musical ability at least was positive as daylight itself. The fame of it spread quickly abroad through that district of scattered farms, in which pianos, acquired sometimes as a proof of 'getting on,' sometimes in the hope of it, were far more plentiful than players; and she had soon no lack of pupils. Many of them would gladly have come to her, but she drily discouraged all such suggested inroads on her seclusion, and chose instead, mounted upon a staid and serviceable old grey horse, to plod her way, all day long and every day, between farm and farm, from pupil to pupil.

A singular choice of life for an elderly woman, and scarcely, one would think, congenial; for nearly all the learners were the most absolute beginners, and their fingers, already past the first suppleness, were coarsened, moreover, with housework; besides which, not one of them, so far as I could discover, ever entertained any musical ambition beyond that of being able to play waltzes and lancers at the monthly socials. Whether this was altogether the fault of the pupils, though, who is to say? By all accounts, Miss Kirkcaldie would not seem to have troubled to bring with her into those farmhouse parlours much inspiration or enthusiasm for her art.

She kept all that for the old kitchen. At dusk, after she had come in from her rounds, had asked, curtly, for her tea, eaten it, and returned the tray, she would put out her lamp and open her piano—and Mrs Callender, eagerly on the watch, would simultaneously open all the doors between the old kitchen and the new: surreptitiously, however! For once, when the passage-door had been thrown open a little carelessly and loudly, Miss Kirkcaldie had instantly arisen, had closed it, with meaning, and had played no more that night.

With that single exception, however, the old kitchen, deserted still by day, now awoke each evening, in the mellow flush and flicker of its own firelight (even in the summer those Southern hills grow cold at sundown, and Miss Kirkcaldie was a chilly soul in more senses than one), to a new and magical existence. Its little humble sphere, heretofore the scene exclusively of practical and actual life, now enclosed experiences neither actual nor practical at all, that were yet exceedingly real. Immortal passions now possessed it, and it sheltered mighty sorrows and consummate joys. Within its homely bound-ary, vast forces impalpably contended; worlds invisible were born; the secrets of the soul declared themselves, and bodiless longings, formless consolations, pulsed and thrilled. Plaintively, imperatively or with despair, the old kitchen re-echoed now the everlasting ques-tions to which there comes never any answer; and all the while was glorious as a chosen home of the undeniable, divine fact—Beauty!

The tears come still into Mrs Callender's eyes when she speaks of Miss Kirkcaldie's music. 'Never,' she says, 'did I hear anything like it. Right through you it went, deep down into your very marrow. Many's the time I've gone an' crept outside that door, an' stayed there shiverin' with the cold—Roger'd be safe in bed—and filled me with the listening till my heart's been fit to break for the grief or glory, or soldierin' or softness, whichever it might be. There! stood there like a silly I have, with the tears a-runnin' down, an' yet all the while as *happy*! Well, there! Someway I used to seem to kind o' wake up, if you understand, when Miss Kirkcaldie made her music. Sour old lemon that she was, too, otherwise!'

It is good to think of Mrs Callender, whose days were else little beyond butter-making, poultry-feeding, and housework, coming into her rightful kingdom of consciousness, as she sobbed and shiv-ered out there in the passage. And it is good, too, to think of that music, like an angel entertained in secret and guarded with jealous pains from bestowing the blessing of its presence upon uninvited guests, yet, true to its heavenly nature, winging thus freely forth and ministering to this refreshed and thankful recipient. But what of the music-maker—the exclusive, haughty host? Nay, poor, proud, solitary soul, why should we give you grudge for grudge, or bitterly estimate your bitterness? Is it so beautiful a thing to condemn where we do not understand? Who knows what stress—of grief, or guilt it may be, of love denied, ambition thwarted, loss sustained (pain of some sort certainly it must have been, to teach your soul such passionate expression)—had driven you to exile and the old kitchen? Who can tell from what sad seed, and planted by what tragic agency, may have sprung that thicket of impenetrable pride that walled you from your fellows as the pine-trees wall the farm?

Nobody, at least in Kiteroa; and perhaps it is as well. It is good at times that curiosity should go ungratified. Miss Kirkcaldie succeeded in remaining a problem to the end. Three years to the very day, after she had drifted into the farm, she drifted away from it again, as suddenly and unexplainingly as she had come. Nobody ever heard where she went to, or anything more about her. The patient bullocks took the boxes and piano-case down the hill again, the cold ashes were swept up from the unrequired hearth, the music was gone, and the old kitchen was shut up once more.

Not for very long this time, however. One scorching day, the summer following Miss Kirkcaldie's departure, it so happened that a couple of young men went strolling out upon the promontory, to get a view of the great Point opposite. The heat gave way suddenly to a violent storm, and they ran for shelter to the farm, which received them hospitably—so hospitably, indeed, that they stayed on there for a week, delighted with their luck. The Callenders, too, were delighted in their turn. Their guests, it appeared, were art-students from town, spending their holiday in a sketching-trip along the coast; and very lively, companionable fellows they proved themselves. It was long since the Callenders had laughed so much—probably, indeed, they had never before found life half so entertaining as it was made that week, by the gay, good-humoured nonsense and sprightly pranks of their guests.

Mrs Callender often referred to them regretfully after they were gone; and it was with the liveliest expressions of delight that one day next spring she read aloud to Roger, who was as pleased as she, a letter from one of them, Mr Martin Mills, imploring her, as the greatest of all possible favours, to put him up during the coming summer, which he proposed to devote to the painting of a great coast scene. He came, accordingly, and was more debonair and delightful than ever. The headland itself was mainly to serve him as a studio, and, unlike Miss Kirkcaldie, he took his meals sociably with his hosts; but the old kitchen was also placed at his disposal, and soon became a sort of miniature *salon*, its brown walls all brilliant with what looked like random bits of sea and sky blown in through the window. And the window itself, too, framed another picture, a live one, the garden in its summer glory—masses of pelargonium, rosy freaked with jet: of snapdragon, soft yellow, crimson and white: azure lupin and larkspur, golden 'glory-cups' (eschscholtzia), and great damask and pink roses: all sprung up bright above their low, cool greenery, and heaped, yet without any crowding or garishness, upon the sapphire canvas of sea and sky. Colour both lapped and lined the little brown room, and it was gay, too, with more than colour. It had company in it now every day, blithe, numerous company, that bubbled over with vivacious chatter, and with airy projects for sports and picnics and all kinds of holiday outings. All the young folk of the neighbourhood seemed with one accord to make for the farm upon the promontory that summer, and many of their elders, too. The Callenders had never been so popular, or had so many visitors; all of whom must pay a visit to the old kitchen, of course, if only to inspect Martin's sketches in the inspiriting company of the painter.

It is doubtful, to be sure, whether the sketches themselves were so very highly thought of. The visitors privately agreed that the young man had a puzzlingly free hand with the facts. That picture of Dicky Jell's house, now—he gave it a gable which it had not got, yet left out altogether the tastiest thing about the whole place; that new verandah-roof painted in stripes of yellow and red, that the Jells were so proud of, and no wonder—it was the latest thing out. But it might still have been in, for all Mr Mills made of it; and though no one, to be sure, could more handsomely have admitted the oversight when it was pointed out to him, still, nobody, either, could have taken less haste to put it right. All the time the picture hung in the old kitchen it was never altered; and Mrs Jell had reason to suspect that it went forth into the world still thus deficient—and could never feel again quite so cordial to the painter in consequence. Mrs Lyon's place, too;—was there really that pool of water before the blue-gums? Of course not! never had been, either. Mrs Lyon herself only wished there was: it would have been so handy for the cows, though perhaps a little rheumaticky, so close to the house, in winter. And there Mr Mills had not only put it in, but actually put *her* in, too, coming down from the door to fetch water! It was almost making the poor old lady act a lie—and, in fact, the chief effect of Martin's art upon his neighbours was to make them realise the far higher veracity of photographs; which came so much cheaper, too.

But whatever might be thought of the paintings, with the painter himself nobody had any fault to find. Before long, Martin was easily the most popular person in Kiteroa, and quite naturally so. To begin with, he was a pleasure merely to look at, with his tall, muscular figure, all ease and buoyancy, his ready, irresistible smile, and happy, kind blue eyes. Then, in addition to good-nature, good humour, good spirits, and a power of enjoyment that was infectious, he possessed an indefinable charm of temperament, 'fluid and attaching,' that coaxed criticism into indulgence and persuaded suspicion to a smile. He was a delightful person; more, he was a delightful person to be with, and that in reality was his chief attraction. Wherever Martin came, a certain sparkle, a peculiarly grateful liveliness, awoke in the company—emanating from him in the first place, certainly, but by no means confined to him. People in his society began to be enchanted with their own, discovering, with a pleasure which in turn naturally helped things on, how bright, how quick, how brilliant they could really be. Martin, in short, was a human effervescent. He was like a spoonful of sherbet, which you have but to slip into a glass of water, and—Presto! how that quiet water does begin to dance! Or, to vary the simile, he was a human sunbeam, not only bringing its own brightness with it, but evoking also a shining answer out of shady places thought hitherto to be all shade. Yes, he certainly was a charming fellow, Martin; and as far removed from his dim, gaunt,

*Blanche Baughan*

dreary predecessor in the old kitchen as the tropics from the pole.

What with the various merrymakings and frolics to which this popularity committed him, the great picture, to be sure, made scant advance beyond the sketches and studies already referred to. But there was plenty of time; for, when autumn came, it appeared that there was an opening for one drawing-class in the little town of Appleby, seven miles away, and another at Hakawai, five miles off in the opposite direction. Kiteroa would make capital headquarters—the roads were good; he would be able easily to ride to and fro—and, to Mrs Callender's great delight (she had already begun to love him like a son), he decided to stay on through the winter.

That was the winter they had the Dramatic Society at Kiteroa. It was in the old kitchen that a merry company of lads, gathered about the great hearth one frosty evening, with Martin as their host, hit upon the captivating idea; it was there that before the eyes of many hilarious and suggesting critics he dashed off those famous flaming sheets of stage scenery; there, too, that he devised costumes, coached the actors in their parts, and conducted rehearsals. The responsible old family *whare* that had taken part in so much life, played at life in those days. At the transmuting touch of Martin, that universal elixir, it became, now a dungeon (with the hanging lamp turned low): now (with the help of Mrs Callender's rocker and two chair-backs) a London drawing-room: now, by mere force of imagination, a ship or a forest, a castle or a street. It is a wonder that its timbers stood the strain. In the course of all this dramatic business, by the way, Martin came to know Avis le Beau.

What with painting, teaching, and the drama, not to mention a whole host of lesser activities, Martin had quite a strenuous life of it at Kiteroa; but all work seemed to come light as a holiday to his buoyant nature. About mid-winter, indeed, he did 'take a week off,' running up (the expression seemed just to fit such an agile temperament) to see his friends in town. But Mrs Callender exclaimed with concern at the white and haggard face with which he returned. He laughed it off, of course: country air and cookery always suited him best, he explained, Kiteroa air for choice and Callender cookery; and he soon picked up again. Mrs Callender feared, however, that there was some hidden delicacy, perhaps of the lungs, about him, and was more than ever fearful of it after he had taken another trip in spring, with the like result; and very glad indeed that he made no plans for leaving Kiteroa, and her unobtrusive cosseting; although it was just then that, for the first time, he fell behind in his payments, which seemed the more singular, since he had taken the sketch with the Jells' house in it, and other pictures, up to town to sell.

And then, alas! soon after his return, a terrible calamity occurred, and a great grief overwhelmed good Mrs Callender. One night Martin did not return from his class at Appleby. He did not come back the next day, either; it was not until the third afternoon that Dicky Jell drove him home in his gig, very dirty and dilapidated, very morose and sick, the saddest possible contrast to the airy, engaging master of the Kiteroa revels. Dicky, it appeared, had found him at the hotel in Appleby, with his credit exhausted, and had brought him away by main force. Alas for merry Martin! The real superiority of Kiteroa air for him over that of town depended, it was obvious, upon its greater distance from a bar.

Poor Martin! And the poor Callenders! They nursed and tended him unreproachfully till he was fully himself again, and then Roger talked to him like a man, and Mrs Callender like a mother. And Martin, true to his lightly hung, easily moved nature, responded to this generous treatment with the utmost readiness. The vituperations that they spared him he heaped on his own head. He swore that he should never forgive himself for having so disgraced, so hurt, such friends. He confessed, with a shame-faced sincerity, that took half the ugliness out of the confession, and disposed its hearers rather to sympathy than blame, that he could not honestly say this was the first time he had so fallen; but he could, and he did, most vehemently vow that it should be the last. It was not, however—neither was the next time, nor the next. Poor Mrs Callender was a woman much to be pitied in those dark days. She was at her wits' end, when Avis le Beau came to the rescue. She married him.

Avis was a practical, capable, resolute girl, her own mistress since the death of her father, and in possession of her own farm. If, as was whispered round Kiteroa, it was really she who proposed the match, that only showed that she had enough sense to see what Martin needed, and enough love and courage to act on what she saw. The neighbourhood, no slower than the average community to throw down its idol from his pedestal, once the feet of clay stood revealed, expressed itself as more than a little aghast at Avis's own prospects. But that was of no moment whatever to Avis once her mind was made up, she was of the kind that would 'stand to be shot.' So she made Martin marry her with the least possible delay and, contrary to all precedent in such cases, she saved him. The fact was, that there was as yet no actual vicious craving in the lad; nothing worse than weakness and a strain of lavish self-indulgence which is bad enough, Heaven knows, but yet is shared by many a man who never actually 'goes wrong.' In Martin's case, it was that very characteristic and charming bonhomie of his that had unhappily played the part of traitor in the garrison; and Avis took him just in time, before tendency had slidden easily and fatally over the brink into habit.

She made him an admirable wife. The firmness of her nature was a staff to his; her courage shamed him, her generosity set his eagerly afire. His responsiveness helped him well with Avis; his ardour and facile-heartedness could be exercised in ever-fresh worship of the wife who had saved him, and his imaginativeness was able to invest her with the glamorous quality she lacked. For Avis, from the crown of her head to the sole of her foot, was purely matter-of-fact; she cared little for beauty, nothing at all for Art. Paint, especially, she considered to be much more usefully and properly bestowed upon gates and weather-boarding than on canvas; it was also contrary to her excellent judgment that any wife should keep her husband. Accordingly, she sold out, and took a farm in quite another neighbourhood, a Prohibition one; and there Martin, who had been brought up in the country, took to farming, made, with her help, quite a success of it, and entirely lived down whatever was amiss in his Kiteroa reputation.

He became, of course, extremely popular in the new

neighbourhood, for that he would be bound to do wherever he went; but whisky never got the upper hand of him again, save once, and that was during the horror of despair—when the first baby came and Avis was pronounced dying. They say it was to a whisper of his condition that she really owed her marvellous recovery; she was so resolved he should be kept straight. Certainly, by her understanding of the needs of Martin the man, she made of him a clear gain for humanity: although whether, at the same time, by her lack of sympathy with Martin the artist, she did not also inflict a certain loss upon it, who shall say? Decidedly, his sketches (there are several of them in the old kitchen still) possessed plenty of breadth and spirit. Martin is happy enough, by all accounts, and at all events his neighbourhood is saved from at least one pied verandah; but I always feel a little rueful and regretful about beauty-loving, beauty-bringing Martin. Avis saved so much, one wishes she could have saved more.

And so the old kitchen lost its transitory brightness, and lapsed into solitude and silence once more. It was scarcely less silent for its next occupant. A certain 'Mr Miller,' a foreigner, had, it appears, in years long since gone by, performed some great service for Mrs Callender's father and mother—that identical young couple who had begun their housekeeping in the old kitchen. Precisely the nature of it, Mrs Callender had never clearly understood; but it had been of the very first importance, and had decisively influenced a supreme crisis in the family fortunes, which had gone on steadily, if modestly, improving ever since. The benefactor's own fortunes, unhappily, had just as steadily pursued the opposite direction; until now in his friendless old age, he was reduced to a most forlorn 'bachelorising' existence in a one-roomed hut near Hakawai. It was in vain that, time after time, Mrs Callender had entreated him to take up his quarters on the farm, and let her, in tardy return for that essential succour long ago, make his declining days as comfortable as she could. No! he always refused, gratefully, but with decision; he had work to do, he said, for which absolute solitude was a necessity.

But when, at length, he and his *whare* grew infirm together; when sinister mention began to be made of the Old Men's Refuge; then, Mrs Callender could stand on ceremony no longer. If Mr Miller himself did not know what was due to the saviour of her father and mother, she did; and accordingly, one fresh and beautiful October morning, when the headland was all soft greens and purples with springing grass and sailing cloud-shadows, she harnessed steady Twinkle into the buggy, and drove off; returning, that same afternoon, with a small, spare, bespectacled man upon the seat beside her, and a quantity of well-packed butter-boxes and flour-bags in the rear. Poor Twinkle seemed to have found his load no light one; and this was not surprising, for the butter-boxes proved to be full of weighty books, and the sacks, all but one, whose leanness hid a few old clothes, were crammed with papers.

Roger, humorously growling, brought them all round by degrees into the old kitchen, now homelike and hospitable once more with a good fire of black-pine, for the sweet spring breeze was keen. But it was not upon the fire that the newcomer's deep-set old eyes fastened themselves with eagerness and brightened as they gazed; it was upon a certain innovation in the room, introduced no later than that very day—some shelves, namely, of plain wood, running along a couple of the walls. He rubbed his veiny, knotted hands together as he looked at them, and before he would so much as glance at the good hot meal Mrs Callender made haste to bring in, he insisted upon unpacking and bestowing on these shelves his beloved books—his 'family,' as he called them with a whimsical smile.

It was a family extremely unlike that other which the old kitchen had known, with fresh, rosy faces and quick limbs; considered, too, as decoration, it could hardly vie with Martin's pictures; for a sorrier, a more blighted collection of volumes can seldom surely have been seen. The backs of many were broken, others could boast of no richer wrapping than was afforded by a bit of brown paper; and the very handsomest members of all faced the world, or rather the old kitchen, in mouldy coats of dull brown leather, sorely scratched and worn. It was possible, of course, that the very sprightliest elegances, the nimblest and most live creations of wit and fancy, might dwell behind these dingy exteriors and be gloomily concealed by them, like comedy behind the curtain; but, if so, the concealment was perfect—the entire library looked to promise nothing lighter than a sermon. There could never be anything in the least fantastic, or light-minded, or gay about the aspect of the old kitchen while it should retain these tenants; but rather, an air of equable responsibility, an atmosphere of grave and even twilight, sobered and somewhat scented, too, by the company of so much unspecious brown leather; and premising, in whatever form of activity should there be pursued, a kind of passionless neutrality, a judicial stability and calm.

As for the human occupant, the father, so to speak, of this un-glittering tribe, he was a gentle and tranquil old man of long past seventy, with a high, shining forehead, and a lofty dome-shaped head, white as a snow-peak in July. He had a mild, absorbed expression; he rarely spoke and even more rarely heard. Mrs Callender had always understood that he was a doctor—*Dr* Miller, her father had always called him—and, the morning after his arrival, before she knew his habits, she coaxed him into the stable to see a poor cow that was down with milk-fever. The old man accompanied her with the most perfect complaisance, gazed at the suffering creature with an air of profound consideration, and lent, or appeared to lend, the most desirable attention to Mrs Callender's painstaking enumeration of its symptoms. But when, at the end, she asked for his opinion, she got a shock; for, slowly shaking that great white head of his, he answered, with a gentle smile, that he had hitherto made it the habit of his life seldom to formulate an opinion, and never to express one—a habit which appeared to Mrs Callender most peculiar in any one, and in a doctor, actively inhuman.

All of a sudden, however, a new idea flashed into her mind—were there not other doctors, as well as doctors of medicine? Of course! and, swiftly seized with a wild and palpitating hope, 'Oh, Dr Miller,' she cried, 'do you—oh, *are* you a musicianer?' at the same time re-volving, with the customary quickness of her woman's mind, all sorts of plans for giving a commission to the very next piano agent who should call. But his answer not only crushed that infant hope past remedy, it also raised a fear; for, 'God forbid!' he said, with an earnestness so devout that Mrs Callender felt her heart almost stop its beating. Could he—oh—could he possibly be a Doctor of—Divinity? Of the habits of such folk she had no experience, it is true, but awful visions beset her—of gentle but persistent admonishings, of sermons on weekdays as well as Sundays. Worst of all, of Roger, at no time an admirer of 'parsons,' and already good-naturedly contemptuous of this poor man who had 'made such a mess of his life,' waxing 'rampageous,' and kicking against the bodily presence of so spiritually minded a ghost. The idea was, indeed, so alarming, that she dared not put it to the proof. The old man had concealed the fact, if fact it were, for so many years, that perhaps, if he were not goaded into declaring it now by ill-judged questions, it might be kept dark still; and she therefore pursued her inquiries no further. She loyally called him 'Doctor,' to the end, however. Failure that he had been, puzzle that he was, mine of danger that he might eventually prove to be, the former bulwark of her father's fortunes should lack nothing she could give him, least of all a title of respect.

Old Mr Miller was very happy at the farm. His original scruples once routed by Mrs Callender's abduction of his person, he never recurred to them—indeed he probably forgot all about them—and accepted her ministrations as naturally, and with as little question as a child. The seclusion of the place suited him well; and in the old kitchen he could enjoy his stipulated solitude without stint. As in its earliest days of all, the old room was now again both bed-chamber and living-room. Once more it enclosed and guarded all the material activities of an entire human life, and provided, with what seemed a peculiar fitness, for the helplessness of him by whose help it had been conserved to the use of its original inmates. The old man became very fond of it; he quitted it, indeed, only for the garden; for he was very shy. The farm itself he never went outside from the day he came to it, and he could never be induced to face any of Mrs Callender's once more infrequent visitors. People, he once explained to her, were like noises, and 'broke his thoughts.'

Of another kind of society, however, presumably less destructive, he was extremely fond—the society, namely, of all the lesser creation, feathered or four-legged, provided only that it was not too big and strong. Perhaps this trait was a mark of that same mercifulness of nature that had sent him to the prompt rescue of the struggling young couple; perhaps it was his portion of the almost universal craving for companionship; or again, perhaps it was what Roger called it, just childishness. Whatever its reason, certainly he treated the smaller and gentler of the creatures about the farm (cows and horses were too big for him, puppies he found too boisterous) after a fashion that their master considered 'clean ridiculous,' and even loyal Mrs Callender in secret thought most trying. For, like the majority of farm folk, these two looked upon animals as nothing at all but bodies, and bodies designed, moreover, for nothing else than to be of use to human owners; while the old doctor went to the other extreme, and gravely regarded them as real personalities, with lives and claims and interests of their own. Understanding, at any rate of the heart, they did undoubtedly possess, he pointed out to Mrs Callender, when Lady, the cattle-dog, deposited one day a still-blind pup between his trusted feet; and he scandalised her severely, on another occasion, by asserting that, in his opinion, the claim of Mab the cat to a soul was as undeniable as her own. Mrs Callender never feared that he was a Doctor of Divinity after that!

But in return, the animals adored their champion; it certainly seemed that there was some real bond between him and them. Mab, before long, had quite deserted the new kitchen of an evening for the old, and Lady, when off duty, would sit quiet by the hour with her nose against the old man's knee, and shared his meals with a regularity that was a further discipline to poor Mrs Callender, who considered, and not perhaps without reason, that her providing was much too good for a dog. The ducks and turkeys, too, would come boldly round the door-step to eat from his hand; and as for the litle fan-tails in the garden, it was really pretty see them with the old doctor. They would come flickering and flirting about his great white head without the smallest fear, and settle on his knee or his finger; cocking their little heads questioningly on one side, and looking up at him out of their bright black eyes with the most knowing expression. When autumn came, they fairly took up their quarters for a time in the old kitchen, creating with their mid-air antics a perfect whirlpool of movement within its quiet atmosphere, breaking the solemn silence with brisk monosyllables of bird chat, and making no scruple whatever, if they wanted a perch, of alighting upon the very most portentous of all the brown leather tomes.

'The lesser brethren,' the old man used to call them; and when Mrs Callender once, humouring him as she would have done a child, asked him what they talked so much to him about, 'Oh, we share a secret,' he answered, with a smile and laying a mysterious finger to his lip. 'Consciousness, men call it, but they know only one word of it. Perhaps the little birds know another.' And good Mrs Callender went sadly away, feeling that Roger was quite right—the poor old dear *was* getting very childish.

As regards his daily life, it was his custom to rise late, and of a bright morning to sit with closed book on his knee—either out on the clean, flagged garden-path between the flower-borders, or else in the streak of sunshine beside his open window. The bees would be humming, the thrushes melodiously busy, and with the fragrance of his morning-pipe (he was a tremendous smoker) would be mingled the freshness of the sea-air and the sweet garden-breath. Suppose the day were chill or wet, he would then seat himself beside the hearth, which Mrs Callender was careful to keep well-supplied with logs; still with a book, and still with that book unopened. It was as though the mere presence of the printed page sufficed him, just as the day's work often goes the better for the mere knowledge that So-and-So is about; or perhaps the contents lived in his memory, and needed no reviving; or, again, perhaps he had another unprinted library in his brain, that it took him all his time to decipher, and the holding of a book in his hand was but a habit, or acted as a suggestion. At all events, he seldom seemed to read.

If the afternoon were fine he would spend some time in pacing up and down among the pines that surrounded it on three sides; by and by he had worn quite a track among them, as Wordsworth's sailor-brother did, home from the quarter-deck. And, after that, he would return to his room, and there sit with his white head sunk on his breast, and his beloved pipe out at last, apparently asleep. Finally, when it was quite dusk, and Mrs Callender had brought in and lit his lamp, 'Doctor Morepork,' as Roger called him to tease his wife, would sit down to the table in the company of pens, papers, and ink, and begin, at length, his day's work. What that work was, constituted yet another puzzle. It was writing, certainly, that was plain enough; but of what kind? what about? Mrs Callender never could discover. Once, in the hope of having wherewithal to glorify him in the eye of Kiteroa, and, if possible, render him a little respectable in Roger's, she ventured to inquire whether he wrote for the papers? 'For the papers!' He repeated the words after her with a scorn, gentle, yet absolute, which, however incomprehensible, proved, at any rate, that he did *not*!

Whatever his mysterious task, however, he worked hard at it. His consumption of kerosene was enormous—although, as Mrs Callender said, she never should be the one to grudge him that, seeing that except for tobacco, which he found himself in, kerosene was about the only thing he did consume; and the sight of his cheerfully streaming window must have heartened many a midnight helmsman off that unlit coast. The old *whare*, that had once presided through the darkness over dreamless slumbers, now kept vigil many a night with this old scholar. Once, in fact, during the summer, Mrs Callender and the sunrise together surprised him in the middle of a sentence—which Mrs Callender stole a look at, by the way, over his shoulder; but, so far from its enlightening her as to the real meaning of all this midnight toil, not one word of it could she so much as decipher. It was all written in some incomprehensible character.

One night, during the winter that followed, she was suddenly awakened—by some kind of cry, she thought, but could not be sure. For a minute or two she lay listening; then, an irresistible impulse drove her to the old kitchen. She found the doctor still sitting at his table, although the clock upon the wall had just struck three; but, for once, he was not writing. All his papers were packed up into one great pile, and this he was holding in his hands, which quivered and trembled about it, and fondled it as though it were one of the little live creatures so dear to him. 'It is done! it is done!' he was exclaiming, almost chanting, as Mrs Callender entered; and she recognised the sound as that which had awaked her.

' What is done?' she asked him; but he did not answer. She could not even be certain that he was aware of her presence, for he had a singular expression, 'as if he was glorying,' and, unwilling to disturb him, she made up the fire softly, and went away. She could not sleep, however; a queer restlessness, a vague feeling of uneasiness, had taken possession of her; and she got up again after awhile, and stole back to the old kitchen. The lamp seemed to have burned low; she turned it up. There sat the old doctor still, and still he clasped his papers. But they were now made up into a parcel, and his head had fallen forward on them. He was dead.

Whether it was legal or not, Mrs Callender never knew, neither did she care; but when she found that the manuscript, whose existence had been so vitally bound up with the old doctor's, was directed to some queer address in far-off Germany, she insisted on Roger's sending it there at once, before the constable came to take over the dead man's affairs. He might refuse to forward it—one never knew; and forwarded at all costs it had got to be, since that was evidently the doctor's last wish. Forwarded accordingly it was, though the postage made Roger whistle and slyly lament to his wife that moreporks were expensive pets. Then Hennessey, the constable, came and cleared away the old brown books, and all the rest of the manuscripts. And, once again, the old kitchen was empty.

No longer ago than last November, I was down myself at the farm on the promontory-tip; and I found Mrs Callender all in a flutter still at the extraordinary event of the week before. Two men had arrived at the farm, two strangers, two foreigners—come all the way from Germany, it appeared, to visit the place where the celebrated Dr Müller (it really was a *ü* in the middle of his name—did I know?) had lived and died, and written his so-famous volume upon… what, Mrs Callender could not for the life of her make out—that had revolutionised… something, concerning which she had been able to gather no idea; except the joyful one that it was so exceedingly important that her father's friend had now become a greatly revered man in his own country. She was very triumphant over Roger about it; but Roger, good, substantial man, stuck sturdily to his guns. Where was the good of a dinner after you were dead? If the poor old duffer couldn't succeed in getting famous in time enough to know it, didn't that show he was a failure, right enough? And, anyway, what the dickens did anybody care for what they thought in Germany about anything?

I went for a minute or two into the old kitchen. It was cool, and still, and shady, although, outside, the garden was blazing-bright already with its early summer bloom; and a great group of Christmas-lilies held up before the window their tall wands of blossomed silver, delicatety detached upon the background of immense blue sea. Two or three brown volumes that had been overlooked by the constable— there had been a couple more, but those Mrs Callender had bestowed in gratitude upon the appreciative strangers—stood yet upon the shelves; a study of the Point done in Martin's most dashing manner, hung over the capacious old hearth; and the tingling silence, as, standing still, I held my own breath in the little breathless space—it was a calm day, and there was no murmur from either pines or sea—felt as though it were holding back some lovely secret of its own, which must presently break forth and tell itself in noble harmonies.

What various lives had been lived in the old kitchen! The young husband and wife and the babies, first, normal as could be; after them, Miss Kirkcaldie the musician, mysterious, aloof, as yonder far horizon; next, Martin the painter, as radiant, as endearing, as evanescent as the summer flowers; and, last of all, the old philosopher with his august white head, sublimely illumined by the flush of posthumous fame as yonder snow-peaks would be soon by the afterglow.

It was strange how the old kitchen seemed to have been chosen from among its compeers in humility, here among the paddocks and the sheep, as a sanctuary for the life that springs, certainly, from the good sound soil of material existence, but wings its way above it; the life that leaves unconcernedly on one side all that is actual, practical, and personal; the detached life of the intellect and of Art.

# PART III

## *Studies in New Zealand Scenery*

# from *The Finest Walk in the World*

Deep in the south-west corner of New Zealand, far away from all familiar scenes of travel, lies the celebrated Milford Sound, an inlet of the sea said to surpass in magnificence even the fjords of Norway. Of late years a track has been made overland to the Sound, and this track anyone possessing feet to walk with, eyes to see with, and a love for Nature at her loneliest and fairest, could scarce do better than essay. It is but some three and thirty miles in length—traversable, therefore, by the practised walker in one day, though very much more profitably allotted two or three: it can be negotiated at any time between early November and late March: a paternal Government has provided it with all necessary accommodation for travellers: and from the variety, the beauty, and the scale, of the scenes through which it passes, it must certainly be accounted one of the most glorious natural wonders of the world.

The Track starts at the head of beautiful Lake Te Anau, and leads at once up a mountain-valley filled with Bush—magnificent virgin Bush, composed mainly of tall 'silver birches,' beeches really (*Nothofagus Menziesii*), whose boughs resemble nothing so much as giant sprays of Titan maiden-hair. Occasionally a single branch holds out a torch of clear gold-yellow, as though Autumn were

> 'Laying here and there
> A fiery finger on the leaves,'

—only, you feel, it must be Autumn in a land of spring, for where is there green fresher than among these evergreens? In early summer, too, the red mistletoe—a parasite, but one that hangs its host with jewels—loves to emboss the birch-boughs with great clusters of bright crimson bloom. A fine day here is a dazzling day; and when, against the brilliant blue of the sky, the generous green of so much foliage glows, and this rich red burns, it is hard to conceive that anywhere there can be light more lavish, lustre more fresh, colour more pure and abundant. The brightness seems to shine into and through you.

[…]

Deep in this forest-cup, whose sides are six sheer mountains, a side-track of mosses and rocks and ribbon-wood glades like an orchard of Kent in flower-time, leads to the highest cataract in the world, discovered by Donald Sutherland before McKinnon found the Pass, and called after him the Sutherland Falls. The highest of the Yosemite Falls, which are divided by a stream, is 1600 ft; the Sutherland's three leaps, which are but one in rainy weather, measure 1904 ft. And how can I hope even to hint at their beauty? From an unseen, glacier-fed lakelet between Mt Daniells and Mt Hart, the escaping current hurls itself straight down the sheer grey mountain-wall, a long, slender, ever-recurring meteor of eager white, received, amid the spray-glittering forest, into an enchanted pool—never quite seen, always mysterious behind its veering veils, elusive, ineludible, of fugitive rainbows, and whirling, evanishing diamonds. There is no such Fall, it is said, and no such setting, anywhere else in the world. It is not hard to believe.

As one stands near the pool and looks up, the highest fall, shooting over the mountain-lip, seems like a white cloud pouring down out of the Blue, and arched like a sea-wave to the plunge… It plunges… vanishes in silver smoke… which then, O wonder! re-ascends toward the sky—as though the spent cloud had a soul, and this was it. But its body then must have gone on falling, for suddenly, out of what must be some deep, hid basin, forth springs the second fall in full career—a long volley of headlong snowy rockets, half of which, midway, are again transformed into vapour floating up. You are near enough to see distinctly these two streams, the one of falling water, the other of mounting mist, continually passing one another, aqueous angels on this Jacob's Ladder of rocks. Then comes the last fall, so much nearer to your eye that you can now feel the pace, the power, of all this perpendicular current. Solidly headed, shining-tailed like comets, down the incessant masses of white water hurl themselves. The grasses on the neighbouring rocks wave wildly; there is continuing thunder, every now and again a heavy roar. But it is not their power that most distinguishes these Falls. Niagara must have a visible force far greater; the Victoria Falls are unmatchable in their union of might and mystery. But the Sutherland has a quality forbidden its compeers by their very mass. It is ethereal, delicate, spiritual almost. Slender, lofty, it comes as if sent down straight out of the sky. That long, swift, snowy insubstantiality, those aspiring breaths of diaphanous amethyst, these airy coils and curves a little solider than smoke, and flying draperies as of molten alabaster—can they really be workaday water at all? At times the whole thing looks less the descent of a stream than a soft floating skyward of mists that know their way. Its fairness is unearthly—but not with the un-earthliness of any Nixie or Undine. Suppose there to be an Angel of All Waters, however, he might really very well be imagined to have taken form here, and be shining secretly out upon the world in the shape of the Sutherland Falls!

[…]

Long, long ago, there was no Milford Sound. Instead, we are told, high up yonder, between the peaks and ridges of the Mitre on one side, of the Lion, Kimberley, and the rest, on the other, a Titan glacier lay, biting icily into its bed. It bit, and bit, and that to some purpose; for to-day you may see the marks of its teeth thousands of feet above the sea-face on which your boat lies rocking, while over a hundred fathom of deep-blue water lie beneath your keel. The glacier has become a canyon, a fjord floored with dark blue sea, and walled with beachless, perpendicular cliffs, that extend far beneath the water, and rise sheer above it from the sea-verge to the snow. The canyon winds, but it is unbroken by any arm or deep inlet; its enormous walls enclose it uninterruptedly for ten miles, and at its narrowest it is less than a quarter of a mile in width. Overwhelming, too, as the impression here of height, is the idea of time; think of the ages required to plough those snows and granite to this sea-inlet! It sounds awful; it *is* awful! yet it is anything but awful only. Here once again we get that true Track note of sharp relief, and harmonizing contradiction; and Milford reveals itself as terrific at once and enchanting, as lovely although colossal. See it by moonlight, all silver and softness! See it at sunset—feet of fire down Pembroke's icy stair, the Barrens steeped in dark rose-red, Mitre Peak gold-headed! Its stern cliffs, beside, are muffled to the tree-limit with warm green Bush, and flushed in summer with the crimson bloom of *ratas*, whose curved boughs, hanging out fearlessly above the sea-waves, paint them as with fire; and the *tui* sings, the fantail flickers, just as naturally and freely within these ice-worn walls as within the tenderest glade of the Clinton Valley; while everywhere they are refreshed and made musical by the incessant cascading of sweet waters. Here and there, to be sure, a landslip has carried away the forest from the sheer face of the cliff, but immediately the creeping mosses, first, have set to work to paint and plant it; then the ferns have come, and the undergrowth is manifestly coming; by and by all will be deep Bush again.

# from *Uncanny Country*

The little blue pool, some two feet perhaps in diameter, that lies upon the bank of the tawny creek, has an extraordinary setting. The most beautiful mosses, the tenderest of ferns, embosom it in soft green, and the whole gully below it and above is filled with the graceful boughs of manuka, feathery and waving; but the pool itself appears to be sunk within a crumpled cushion of bright tomato-red plush, and the little stairway, as it were, that leads from it down into the creek, is of the same startling hue, and ends, moreover, in a vivid splash of strong orange-chrome. It is all a bit of barbaric beauty; its aspect is positively sensational. But its aspect is not the most sensational thing about it. As you stand looking, all of a sudden the shining sky-blue water of the pool turns to white, snow-white; the richly-coloured incrustation now surrounds hillock upon hillock of struggling foam, first climbing, climbing up out of it, next apparently pulled strongly back from below: while, down that unbelievable stairway, a spasmodic cascade of the clearest water begins to pulse and spring towards and into the creek. Next moment, the hillocks subside, the cascade ceases; a veil of white vapour hangs gauzily before the face of the pool, then, rising, floats away among the manuka-sprays; and the green glen about the blue pool and glaring streak of colour is quiescent as before. Until, at the top of the cliff just across the creek—a cliff apparently composed of bosses of rose-pink coral—something else begins to happen. Out of a sideway fissure, first great fumy blue breaths come fitfully volleying: next, in the midst of them, sprays and fountains of clear water are tossed up, six feet perhaps into the air: they sparkle in the sun—they dwindle, fail—next they have vanished. But now what is taking place in the little basin at the foot of the pink-coral cliff? The water there, tinted like a sapphire,

inconceivably clear, and apparently unfathomable, seems actively
to be boiling; and up through its depths of colour, flashes of bright
lightning—or are they broad silver fishes?—leap towards the surface,
where, amid an ebullience of bubbles, they suddenly—are not! And
the same thing, alternatively with an outbreak of white climbing
hillocks, keeps happening again within yet another basin hard by: a
basin this time of colour exquisitely harmonious, where the bright
clear water swims within an inner bowl of velvety blackness, and
the outer border, of faint fawns and pinks and mouse-colour as soft
as smoke, melts suddenly at one side into a wash of pure old-gold.

What and where is this strange place? It is a square yard or two
of the Geyser-Valley of Wairakei; and it lies in the North Island of
New Zealand, in the heart of what is there known as the Thermal
District. A singular district: stretching, in a strip some twenty miles
broad by a hundred and fifty long, through the heart of the island:
terminating at its southern end in the snows of Ruapehu and the
smoking cone of Ngauruhoe, at its northern, in the hollow burning
crater, twenty-eight miles out to sea, that is called White Island:
and including within its area countless phenomena as spectacular
in appearance, as sudden and spasmodic in energy, and in essence
as inscrutable, as the Red Geyser and the Dragon's Mouth, which
furnished us, a few lines back, with an introduction to their family.
It is not a beautiful country, although it contains beauties. In the
main, it consists of a high tableland of pumice soil, stretching out
sad-coloured miles—for little at present grows upon it but the thin
grey greenery of 'tea-tree' (manuka) scrub—between the many broken hills and mountains that crop out oddly upon it. But here and
there columns of white smoke glitter up out of the scrub, and cliffs of
bright-hued earth diversify the dulness of the landscape; while, upon
a nearer view, the whole surface of the region is found to be pitted
and perforated by the operations of a certain curious energy, and
the region itself, upon a closer acquaintance, invested with a certain
curious glamour. Centuries ago, as the presence of half-a-dozen
extinct volcanoes and the prevalence of the pumice soil abundantly

attest, it was in the various forms of volcanic action that this line of weakness in the earth's crust, this insufficient lid, let through some of the ever-restless forces below. But, gradually—why, who really knows?—those unthinkable forces have grown less forceful, and the manifestation of their still-surviving energy has consequently changed its nature. The spouted flames and rocks have quieted down now to spouted vapours and water;—yet how mysterious these later fountains are, and how busy is that quietness! Sprinkled at large all up and down its length and breadth, gathered together here and there into special centres and congregations, the innumerable host of these strange little individual activities—these hydrothermal phenomena, to give them their due designation—makes this strip of New Zealand unique. There is not any known form of their peculiar energy which it cannot exhibit. There is no similar zone in the world which can excel, at any rate for variety and abundance, its crowd of curiosities.

[...]

Unless the White Terrace at Orakei-Korako be the one exception, no true terrace-pools now remain to the Thermal Region. There are, however, two pools with very remarkable sinter slopes, rippled if not terraced—the Champagne Pool, namely, of Waiotapu, and the Champagne Cauldron of Wairakei. Of these, the first, a large, and very excitable pool, easily irritated into actual effervescence by the mere throwing in of a handful of earth, sends its overflow gushing down a very gradual slope, which it has carpeted with a smooth sinter, resembling, both in surface and colour, ivory velvet glimmeringly brocaded, by the interplay of sunbeams and shallow ripples, with a myriad shining threads of silver. The slope ends, too, in a charming little cascade of water, cooled by its journey and therefore unveiled for once by steam, flowing down a cliff of creamy silicate—the whole effect gratefully gentle to the eye and with a pretty name: the Primrose Falls. The other Champagne Pool, that of Wairakei, is certainly one of the most really delightful of all the present thermal sights. It lies, not far from the Red Geyser, in a chasm of the glen-side, crowned with fern and walled with waving manuka; and you take your stand, if you are so fortunate, some bright sunshiny morning, upon the opposite cliff—of pinnacled and pitted rose-red earth, richly velveted with emerald mosses, plumed with a thousand tiny jets of bright white smoke—and look down, across the creek, upon a wonderful scene. At first, we will hope, all is vapour—vapour milky, opalescent, veering hither and thither. Now it dissipates for a moment, ascends… you catch a glimpse… but, instantly it is back. Again it is gone… again returned… and so again and again; but by degrees your eye at last has gleaned and gathered in the complete picture—verified perhaps by the mist's whole momentary clearing—of a broad, shallow slope, descending towards the creek from the hillside, and out of a great and clean-white volume of smoke whence at intervals there comes a loud voice roaring. The slope is very smooth, and looks for the most part as though it were composed of ivory or white marble; but here and there it is stained with amazing quantities of amazing colours— orange-gold, old-gold, rose-colour, dull pink, the green of malachite, the puce of plums—that seem to have come cascading headlong down it, or flowed broadly out upon it in random washes, and so to have stayed; and here and there it is set with pools like jewels. Aquamarines they resemble mostly, and opals; but one, set at one side of the slope, within a fern-rimmed bowl of brown-and-crimson earth, is of a beautiful soft raspberry hue; and the sinter between it and the creek is enamelled with a runnel of old-rose between old-gold borders. The whole slope or terrace, too, is brightly intersected, from cloud to creek, by a chain of flowing crystal pools, aquamarine again in colour, and of a clearness so absolute, that, even from this distance above and from them, you can see within their depths what looks like some rich formation of white coral—the petrified remains, in reality, of many a manuka-twig. This living girdle of gems gives off a light breath—now and again it pulses visibly, reinforced with a fresh flow from behind the curtain beyond it of white cloud. Ah, but now, see! the breeze has caught that curtain, has drawn it aside—and, between the sharp white lip of the terrace, and the hill-cliff at the back, there is revealed, for an instant, a great, deep-blue pool. Fifty or sixty feet it actually is in diameter, but you will rarely, if ever, see the whole of it at once; the vision of it is a fleeting one; knowledge of it must be snatched piecemeal. Now, for example, on the left, you can descry two fountains, not very large,

'Columns and cones of boiling snow,'

thrusting up out of the dark blue… then vanishing in the mist. Now, on the right, behind an outjut of rock, there appears, with a violent roar, as it were the brightness, dimly seen, of some great white body, rising up waist-high out of the pool, with a spreading of the hands, so that all the surface of the water crisps to little curls and crimps of white… then, instantaneously, all is whirled away again out of sight by a sudden ascension of the dense white cloud. And, all the while, warm airs come and go; the murmuring manuka-branches drowsily wave and wave, the sound of many waters mingling lulls your ear. You may very well, especially if you are without human company, feel yourself becoming entranced, as you stand and watch, there below you—now eclipsed, now enhanced, by the soft, involving veils, now lit with sudden sun, now all pale mist—the beauty of this strange scene: brightening, swaying, swooning—vanishing yet still there; a dream, yet real; a part of Nature, yet, in effect, sheer magic.

# from *A River of Pictures and Peace*

Once upon a time, says an old Maori legend, two brother mountains, whose home was near Lake Taupo, in the centre of the North Island of New Zealand, both fell in love with a maiden mountain living near. The names of the brothers were Taranaki and Tongariro; Pihanga was the name of the maiden; and Pihanga and Tongariro you may see to this day near Lake Taupo still; but not Taranaki. For Taranaki was the lover who longed in vain; and, wild with grief and anger, he tore himself up by the roots, and left his home, plunging recklessly through gully and hill and forest until he reached the sea; and then he went a little way north, and stopped where you may now behold him seated all alone, and the *pakeha* calls him Mt Egmont. But a long way of woe he had left behind him, and a long jagged wound upon the bosom of Papa, the Earth; for as he went, he had rent the hills asunder, and cloven the forest in twain; sore was the road of his sorrow. But, from the side of Tongariro that he had left, there welled forth presently a river of sweet water; and this river followed the footsteps of Taranaki as far as to the sea; and by its flowing the wound was cooled and the grief comforted, so that the ferns and the forest grew again. And flowing still is this river; and the name of it is Whanganui.

The *pakeha* puts the matter much more prosaically in his geography books. All he says is that the river Wanganui rises on the slope of Mt Tongariro, and for some two hundred miles flows westward, to the Tasman Sea, through a deep, narrow rift caused by an earthquake. Choose which explanation you will! the fact, which is the river, remains the same—a furrow of former violence that has brought forth peace, an old road of ruin that has become a highway of beauty. The Wanganui is in fact the loveliest of all the longer rivers of New Zealand; and it is linked, too, with the history of both the brown man and the white, and in addition possesses a charm that is all its own. May we then visit it together for a little, you and I?

[…]

Meantime, let us turn our eyes to something that upon the Thames we certainly never should see, and that is—our native fellow-passengers. See that old man there, tall, well-built, not tattooed—there is no tattooed man along all the river to-day—no darker than many a Spaniard, and tidily dressed in European clothes… yet with the Maori triumphantly topmost still, in that fine long pheasant's feather decking his bowler hat! The girl at his side, with a great striped shawl gathered round her, and a little black-eyed baby inside it, on her back, and nodding out over one shoulder, has tied a kerchief of bright new rose-pink silk over her rippling raven locks, and persuaded her feet into a pair of openwork stockings and new yellow shoes that positively illumine the deck; but her appearance is quite eclipsed by that of the handsome matron opposite. *Pakeha* is the cut, Maori the amplitude, of that moss-green velvet coat and skirt! The lady's blouse, of Tussore silk, hangs beltless; her hat is an erection, in the latest style, of milliner's roses; she wears one earring, composed of a large shark's tooth, which is mounted in red sealing wax, and tied to the ear with black ribbon; and at her neck there dangles a magnificent pendant of greenstone, probably a very ancient and valuable heirloom. What is she pulling out now from those rich recesses of her coat? A little black pipe! which she fills, with aplomb, and smokes, with enjoyment; and then, putting it carefully back, she draws out a little beautifully-embroidered white handkerchief, and wipes her beautifully-tattooed mouth. There is a real 'Maori lady of the transition period' for you, if you like!

[…]

At first, it is the beauty of the details that one realises. As we glide along the foot of the cliff, we can look down at the little plentiful maidenhair that dips itself into the water, or up, into the little faces of purple and white flowers, the freshness of ferns innumerable, and the darkness of overarching boughs. We can peer into the little black secret chines, that here and there like knife-cuts rend the cliff from top to bottom; discover the hiding waterfalls within, and with the spray breathe in their delicious fragrance of moist leaf and moss and fern—true breath of the Bush. Or we can look across at the opposite cliff with all its laces and embroideries of green, and into the noble, many-folded forest above—dark with *rata*, with birches, with spiring *rewa-rewa*, *tawa*, *tawhai*, and light with whole acres of tree-ferns. The tree-ferns! Stately, tender, bright, theirs is a dominant motive in the Wanganui symphony. Here and there a single specimen springs out above the water—a princeling of the forest, with its slender, frondless stem some thirty or forty feet in height, and its great green drooping coronet keeping the sky from us like an umbrella. But up there, massed together on the hillside, the stems all hidden, and the crowns set closely side by side, they look like encampments of fresh fairy pavilions, and their lively green breaks in upon the darkness of the tree-tops like a laugh. On a dull day they make you think that the sun has come suddenly out; and in autumn or winter they lend the riverside the gay glad hue of spring. Nor is this the only relief that Colour can afford the forest; in January these sombre *ratas* are pyres of crimson bloom; in October, those mist-like *kowhai* boughs burst into abundant golden rain, and the snowy clematis hangs in the tree-tops like a morning mist that has forgotten to melt. At all seasons, there is variety, and luxuriance indescribable, for this is the true North Island tangle.

# from *Summit Road*

Rising suddenly up from a corner of the Canterbury Plains, the Port Hills rear for miles along the sky their tawny, semi-circular rampart of rocky and jagged crests, and send down into the flat a succession of long, tawny spurs, enclosing long, tawny-green valleys. Their fantastic sky-line suggests at once a volcanic origin; and they really are, in fact, the outlying spurs of Banks Peninsula, that odd, volcanic excrescence upon the east coast of the South Island of New Zealand. The height of them reaches sometimes to an altitude of nearly two thousand feet; it is never less than one thousand; and close to their summits all the way, truncating only some of the higher peaks, overlooking now the Harbour, now the Plains, runs the smooth and easy track known as the Summit Road. It leads from the lighthouse at Godley Head to Cooper's Knob—a distance of some eighteen miles in all; but it can be reached from the flat at various points in its career—and strike it where you will, what a walk it offers! Everywhere it is well-graded, in places almost level; its air, coming from whichever way fresh from snows or sea, is so light and pure, so brisk and invigorating, that five miles along the summit of the hills seem no more than one mile on the flat; and then—the view!

Different points along the route yield of course different prospects; but the main effect is everywhere the same—that of a mighty panorama, commanding at once, and liberating, eye and mind alike. Hundreds of feet below, the vast plain of Canterbury, flat apparently as any sea, criss-crossed with hedges, dotted with trees and homesteads, and chequered green and brown by cultivation, spreads itself wide out beneath an enormous sky. Southward, that is to the left as one stands looking, the plain flows on apparently for ever; northward it meets, by means of a beautiful great crescent curve of yellow sand,

the further plain, blue and shining, of the sea; within it not far from
the coast, amid dark bouquets of trees and glitterring curls of smoke,

'A sounding city, rich and warm,'

to adapt the words of John Davidson,

'Smoulders and glitters in the plain,'

with a river shining beyond; and, then, as if all this were not enough,
forty miles or so across it, facing the beholder, there stands superbly
a huge, magnificent wall of mountains, parallel with the plain, and,
stretching beyond it out to sea as far as the eye can reach: range
behind range, shoulder above shoulder: based upon purple, shad-
owed with blue and bronze, crowned, and fully clothed in winter,
with pure white.

[...]

It is the smoke, too, that links the pictorial value of the city with
its vital importance to the scene. This New Zealand Campagna has
but little human history as yet. Apart from a few, all too few, tales
of the Maori warriors who held it once, its one human event so far
is the coming of the white man, and his founding here in 1850, of
that four-square little city, which he intended should represent in
the New Land the best social and ecclesiastical traditions of the Old.
It has, however, already long outgrown these first dimensions and
aspirations both; and if there is not yet much history made by the
city, her human, nay, her cosmic, importance to the scene is already
very considerable. Some people are squeamish about man's interfer-
ence with Nature; and some of her pictorial effects he may, he does
undoubtedly, spoil; but her poetical, her universal aspect—that,
how enormously he enhances! The presence of the Cape-to-Cairo
railway bridge, for instance, amid the very spray of the Victoria Falls,
takes nothing away from Nature's impressiveness, but emphasises it,
instead—by setting next to her own triumph of 'inanimate' creation,
the triumph of that co-partner of hers—man. So here, the presence

of our city in the plains, I will not say lends them a soul, since a soul in their own right I am persuaded they have already—but it vivifies them in another sense. Visibly breathing, doing, making, there it lies, what a reservoir of change! How many actions, how many feelings, how many thoughts, far-reaching, immortal, and ever active all, are at this moment coming, down there, to the birth! 'The joyful and the sorrowful are there; men are dying there, men are being born; men are praying—on the other side of a partition, men are cursing... Friend, thou seest here a living link in that tissue of History, which inweaves all Being.' Yes, Teufelsdröckh would have enjoyed this view of Christchurch from the Summit Road.

# PART IV

*People in Prison*

# Roderick Dhu

It was a girl prisoner, who had known him 'outside', that introduced me to Rod. '*Do* get hold of him,' said she, 'for he's got such a lot of good in him. But everybody's down on him and he's always in trouble.' This was only a woman's judgment and I soon found out what the 'whole round world' thought. 'What, *him*? Don't touch him, he's a rascal, he's a young wretch, he's hopeless!' cried one friendly and experienced official after another; and I daresay they would claim to this day, if any of them survive, that events proved them right. For my part, I can never be thankful enough that I did 'touch him'. There are worse things in life than pain, and there are few things we can so ill afford to forget as the memory of a stout, a loyal and a generous spirit.

The girl pal had evidently managed to give me the right 'password', for my very first letter—Rod was imprisoned in a distant town—showed that confidence had been established. The reply was immediate, in a blotted boyish scrawl written in a large round hand. The whole thing reminded me of nothing so much as the tempestuous onset of a puppy called by name, after being lost, and starved, and badly bruised. And very like a pup, in lots of ways the writer of that letter proved—a really good pup, too, with plenty of points. Wild and reckless he was, all growls and teeth at the merest glimpse of 'the boot,' and abominably mis-trained from birth. But withal, spirited, strong, very intelligent, and deeply affectionate.

'I'm glad to say,' he cried, in that first reply of his, 'that I have never had a letter like yours before in my life—it hadn't a word of religion in it.' He had been deluged, it appeared with 'religious letters' and Testaments; now he turned eagerly towards the hope of 'a real friend.' 'My idea of a friend,' he wrote when asked for a definition, 'is a person whose society is congenial to me at all times, one who understands one's mind and disposition at all times, one that would not desert you at a crisis, in short, who would stick through thick and thin. This is my idea of a friend. I have ony had one friend like this. When we were apprentices on the same ship together his trouble would be mine and mine his. It was our first trip to sea. He died, poor chap, off East Africa. I thought I should have died, too. I wish I had, it would have saved myself and other people lots of trouble.'

His 'history' was rather unusual. His family, in Old England, was quite well-to-do and he had had a Grammar School education till he was fourteen. Then, on his own demand, he went to sea. From a worldly point of view he had had 'every advantage,' but behind the good school was a bad home. Asked once concerning his mother— 'She hated me,' he blurted out—'she drank, that's why I never touch the stuff.' His father, moreover, idolising his only son, gave him too much freedom and far too much money. So it came that a sensitive and difficult boy was left without the most 'socialising' of all influences—mother love—and was thrown back upon a father who sought to restore the balance without discretion or discipline. The mature age of fifteen found Rod ashore by himself in a foreign land, with plenty of cash and 'friends'—of a sort. Soon, without cash or friends, he was at sea again, drifting hither and thither, until at the age of eighteen he arrived in Dominia. Deserting his ship, he found himself, within three months, for the first time in his life, in a Court and charged with stealing. 'And I *had* stolen, too,' he admitted. 'I couldn't find work, I didn't know anyone, and I couldn't beg.'

Now, most unfortunately, on this, the threshold of his career of crime, Rod was the victim of a grave blunder on the part of the administration of justice. He was mistaken for a certain 'crook' who was 'wanted' at the time; and he was clapped into gaol for three years with the brand 'incorrigible.' He was, you will remember, only eighteen years of age, and his own offence merely the petty theft of a lad driven to desperation. It has been stated that the mistake was discovered, but could not be put right. Neither at this stage, however, nor at the first hearing, was legal advice available. The sailor lad knew nothing of the 'rights of accused persons', and it was nobody's business to inform him. He was, as so many are under such circumstances, utterly confused, and so was left to certain conviction and committal to one of those clean and tidy 'schools of crime' which in Dominia are called Prisons.

Rod was an apt pupil and he quickly graduated. He went in an 'accidental' offender. He came out a determined criminal, a criminal by conviction—in more senses than one.

Smarting from disgrace, maddened by injustice, he threw himself, while in prison, whole-heartedly upon the side of those 'enemies of society' to whom society had so carelessly introduced him. He learned how to steal better, so that he might the better 'get his own back' or 'get evens' as these men say. To these 'comrades' he transferred all his abundant stock of loyalty. 'If you *will* call me a pig, then you can be sure I'll act like one,' I once heard a schoolboy of just Rod's stamp say to his sister; and for nine years this lad did, in fact, live the life of a criminal and outlaw. 'It doesn't matter how I succeed in the future,' he explained to me, 'I shall always have the prison stigma. This is why I have not thought it worth while to straighten up. It is all very well for some to say "what rot," people who say this kind of thing should be made to go through the experience and see.'

'If, when I got out,' he wrote later, 'anything began to be missed, what sort of a chance do you think I should have? Guilty or not, it would be "Good night, Nurse," for about five or six years.' (Oh, tragic prophecy!) 'The sneak and the liar I see more of here in one day than I suppose *YOU* do in a year, but still they are only human beings. I sometimes despise myself for despising them. If I had had the nerve to cadge off someone when I first came to this country I shouldn't have been in here to-day. Anyway, I'd sooner do what I did than be a cadger.'

Christmas drew near, and he wrote—'I wonder if you could get permission for me to take up a collection among the boys here— to give a good time to some poor unfortunates at Christmas time.

Christmas is a very awkward time for people who have no friends or money or home to go to. First time I was released I was in a similar position, and I should know.' He had alas! discovered how sketchy are Dominia's ideas of after-care for the released convict.

Our friendship prospered. He seemed a manly fellow, a regular rollicking Jack Tar, such a schoolboy and so independent, that by and by another characteristic came upon me with something of a shock. I was later than usual with my letter, and he was heart-broken. 'You haven't written!' he wrote, and then humbly, 'Have I said anything to hurt your feelings? I would not hurt your feelings for the world.' The same sensitive heart is shown in another letter. Old Mrs D. 'and her sport of a daughter' had visited Rod as well as William. ' Miss D.,' he says, 'tells me she hasn't heard from you for a long time, so I told her I would ask you to write to her. You will, won't you, even if you have to miss me.' … 'She has a bad cold and she didn't look at all like herself,' he added compassionately.

By this time the leaven of 'being understood' was working strongly. 'I woke up this morning and said to myself—Rod, old chap, many happy returns of the day! I am twenty-eight, getting on, eh? And just as silly as ever … This is the ninth birthday in here, and the last. What a great deal has happened to me in this one short year. I remember that first letter of yours, the surprise I felt … It is just wonderful what knowing that somebody really does care what becomes of one will do for one.'

I learned from other sources that his conduct was changing rapidly. He had dropped swearing and 'looking for trouble.' In due course this reacted on the prison treatment. 'I have been moved,' he writes, 'from the strong-rooms to a first-class cell—It makes one feel that he can be trusted and I can see the need of discipline, too. I could see that a year ago but couldn't stand it at any price. Now I don't know half my time there is such a thing.' Then proudly, 'I have not had a bad mark for twelve months.'

Loyalty to his mates, bred of common suffering, remained, however, unshaken. Three men in that prison were in correspondence with me at the time, and a fourth, Cornelius, had announced to them that he was going to do the same, and 'work' me, on release, for his own ends. The reactions of the three to this were characteristic. All felt that I should be warned, but they were all hampered by the Prison censorship of letters. William gave me a cautious—'Be very careful with C.' Flamboyant 'Young Lochinvar,' only suppressing the man's name, laid bare the whole 'vile plot' with a flourish, vastly enjoying his role of 'Hero protecting a friend.' It was Rod who produced the following, 'I want your advice on a matter that has been worrying me … Supposing you had a friend and you esteemed him very much, one who did what he could for all unfortunates. Suppose we call him F.—and suppose there's another, C.—an acquaintance, who, to your knowledge makes plans to abuse F's friendship. Would you think it your duty as a friend to make the facts known to F? I happen to find myself in this position and, you see, I rather shrink from the idea of doing it—I don't think I could do a fellow-prisoner a bad turn if I tried.'

No, he couldn't, as he proved afterwards. At the time he was mightily relieved to be told that 'F. knew enough to be safe from victimisation.'

At last came the jubilant cry. 'I can go out on parole! You cannot imagine how I feel about this, and how grateful I am to you and Mr A. (the governor). At first I felt like crying and then laughing. Oh, I can't explain how I felt properly—Mr. A. said, "H'm, I told you you could work out your own salvation"—It just goes to show how sympathy and understanding will bring the best to the surface in most of us, doesn't it? I hope I never get like I was a year ago again. It was just terrible. I used to think everybody was my enemy. I was just embittered, but know better now.'

In one letter, referring to the foolish act of another, he does a necessary bit of discriminating about 'sympathy.' 'I did the same thing once, I only did it out of sympathy, but I found it wasn't the right kind of sympathy, either for myself or the other person.' It was a lesson much needed by his hot heart. If only he had lived to learn it more thoroughly!

Well, out he came, went straight, and went forward by leaps and bounds. He found a job, earned the liking and respect of his work-mates, and after only a few months, won the love of a good girl. But the shadow of those nine wasted years was over him. You, who live without molestation under the protection of the 'law,' what do you know of 'being hounded' by it? You, who look upon prisoners merely as enemies of Society, being 'justly punished' for their crimes, how can you know the social stunting which may come of those years of prison-training? You, whose loyalty is with the hunter, how can you understand the loyalty which binds together the hunted?

It is not possible to develop any human being normally in prisons, places, however clean and ' healthy,' which keep the victim away from the opposite sex, from children, from the sick, and from all the tenderer, socializing emotions, places which shelter him too, from all responsibility and initiative. He is not called upon to face emergencies and choose lines of conduct, and so to develop judg-ment, resource and social understanding. You may keep him in the very best cold storage—and in Dominia we pride ourselves that we do—but he cannot grow socially, and very often he doesn't really 'keep.' He simply goes bad.

My friend Rod, when he came 'out,' was, mercifully, sound at heart; but he was also still exactly at the same crude boyish stage of social development at twenty-eight as he was when he went 'in' at eighteen. He was still boyishly 'cheeky,' boyishly reckless, keen on brilliant socks and ties, totally ignorant of the value of both time and money. He was wanting in that social wisdom which was especially demanded by his social handicap. After a year came a slack season with no work and much discouragement. Then came an old prison-mate; and the shadow fell.

A crime was attempted in the neighbourhood. Nothing was actu-ally stolen, but the police had, of course, a watchful eye on Rod and a piece of circumstantial evidence enabled them to fasten upon him as the probable culprit. He protested his innocence, but was arrested and at his trial his old 'record' was produced, and made to bear witness against him. Society once more condemned him. 'I've always been guilty before, but now they're going to bring me in guilty when I'm innocent!' was his horrified whisper in Court after the Judge's summing up, a summing-up which, clearly based upon past convictions, left no hope. The Jury brought in a verdict of 'Guilty,' and the Judge responded with a savage sentence of many years.

We said Goodbye at the Courthouse. 'You didn't do it, Rod?' I asked in a moment of privacy. Eye to eye he answered instantly, 'Of course I didn't!' with a deep full look of indignation that is burned upon my heart. I can at least be thankful that he knew that I believed him.

He hanged himself in his cell next morning. Beside the body lay a pencilled note written on bits of paper and addressed to me. 'By the time you get this,' it said, 'I shall be no more on earth. I know you will say I have no right to take my life, but I am going to see what is beyond. You have some idea of the life I have led the last twelve months. I do not want you to go to any more trouble or expense in trying to find N. M.—(the actual culprit)—let him have his liberty, for though I am innocent of the charge brought against me, I do not see why two should suffer. Tell Judge B.—although he is a Judge he is liable to make mistakes and he did so in my case … Give Sally the watch-chain and tell her to keep it in memory of one who thought more of her than life. Well—thank all the friends that have helped you in my case and I shall be thinking of you and S. to the last, so goodbye both of you, let us hope we shall meet in the next world. Do not think I am mad, I am quite sane.'

What a hardened villain he sounds, doesn't he?—this lad who, robbed of all that makes life worth living, has yet no rancour for his robbers, only a heart full of love for his friends, and, to the bitter end, loyalty to a disloyal prison-mate.

Years later, while serving another sentence, that prison-mate confessed, partly to the Chaplain and to another, how he had managed to incriminate Rod.

'Since his arrest,' wrote one who knew him, 'men who have lived and worked with him have come and told me what a decent chap he was, no sneak, clean minded and clean-mouthed about women, absolutely sober, and very anxious to get work—which was not easy, for he had never had a thorough training at anything.' The straight, good and loyal girl to whom he had given his heart wrote, 'He was the best boy I ever went with.' For my own part, and I have had him freely at my house, I have known hundreds of men who have never been in prison that were not half as decent as Rod. But he had been branded 'criminal' and nobody would hear, at the end, of his being anything else.

Read again from those early letters. Exactly what he had antici-pated had come true.

In sober reality, none of his crimes against Society had been very great. They were never vile or indecent—never directed against the person. Nor did they cost us in hard cash, taken all together, what some 'respectable,' but profiteering, business firms cost the com-munity in a month. 'I'm not even a good thief,' he once told me with a rueful grin. 'I've never scored, in all, so much as the price of one decent suit.'

What, on the other hand had Society done against him? It had sent him to prison for his first venial offence. It had provided him, for his sole companions, other and worse law breakers, among them, eventually, the one who wrought his final ruin. Of a wild, reckless, impetuous boy—nothing worse—it had thus sedulously manufac-tured a wild, reckless, and impetuous criminal. For all that energy, spirit, pluck, loyalty, capacity for affection and deep feeling, it found no use at all. During all the time, nine whole years, that Dominia's penal system had held him in its grip, during, in fact, the whole of his young manhood, it had never taught him thoroughly one useful, socially-accepted trade, while it had, on the contrary, supplied him with an expert's knowledge of illicit ways of gaining a living. The penal system, whatever its pretence, had never attempted to 'reform' him. It had noted only what was bad in him—it had never inquired into what was good or what might be developed into something better. It had crippled his growth as a human being. It created the handicap—the last hurdle which brought him down—when the punishment for his first real offences was over.

Was that punishment, indeed, ever over? Was the shadow ever allowed to lift? In the closing scene, at the first breath of suspicion, Society condemned him at once, clapping him in gaol on remand, and publishing matter well calculated to poison any jury's mind, long before trial. At that trial, it would allow no weight to any of the good proved, in his year of liberty, to be in him, and to be growing. I have often thought how, if the Judge had treated Rod as you or I would treat any lad of ours who had appeared to lapse in process of overcoming a bad habit—if he had said, 'Well, you seem to have been trying, and that is certainly something, I'll give you a chance,' if this had been done—how all his generosity would have leaped to the occasion and how safe for evermore would Society have been from any danger at his hands!

Well, Society chose a very different way of safety for itself. For the second time, it made about him so terrible a mistake that it brought upon him despair of human justice, despair of human good-will. It proved to him that he could never hope to win any place in this world except as the criminal it had trained him so well to be. It took from him every chance of doing better; it removed every motive for striving by showing him that he would never be given any chance to live and love like others; it killed in him the very will to live. Was it only Rod's own hand that took his life? Are Society's quite clean?

Rod outgrew his enmity and ill-will to Society. Has it, as yet, outgrown its enmity and ill-will towards such as he?

## Cherry and Co.

Now we approach my second group—the non-normal.

'*Cherry* would like to be a good boy, if he could!' a colleague once observed to me, and it was true. But was Cherry good? Mercy—no! By his record he was incorrigible, and his latest crime had been the rape of a child! *Why* wasn't he good? Why couldn't he be? The answer is that he was a friendless half-wit.

'What is this?' the intelligent reader will object. 'Surely Dominia does not treat mentally deficient offenders as though they were responsible ones? Surely she does not send them to gaol when their offences are caused by infirmity! Surely when the sentence is served these infirm are not again let loose without steps taken to protect Society—and themselves—from the repetition that is otherwise sure to follow?'

It is not pleasant to place the fact on record against one's own State, but such is the senseless, uneconomical, cruel fact. She has no Homes for her grown-up feeble-minded. She lets them marry, too, and only recently has begun to take any thought about their children. The idea of dealing with such a matter at its source has not yet occurred to her. The half-wit with friends does not fare so badly, but the poor and friendless drift in and out of gaol, a sorry flock and sad. Irresponsible as the 'banana-babes', homeless, and at the mercy of their impulses, they are mostly as affectionate and docile as the pauper-spirits. While 'in', they are the butts and cats' paws and victims of those much worse than themselves. 'Out', they are nobody's business, more hopeless, more helpless and more dangerous, a most miserable burden on the community of whose foolish ignorance they are the victims.

Take Cherry, for example. Nothing is known of his early history, except that his father deserted him and that he is not a native of Dominia. When we first met he must have been in the early twenties, a poor little shrimp of a boy who had, however, already been able to serve the community by stopping a bullet with his body in the Great War. He was not at all the wild beast his 'list' had led me to expect; but, 'under custodial care,' very meek and biddable, and easily taught that smattering of trade, which, even at their best, is all our prisons can teach. But alas, he had been put, of course, with the 'rank and file', and by them was also taught worse things. Once you knew Cherry you could very readily understand his offences, and see that they could and should all have been prevented. He was, like so many of the feeble-minded, not at all feeble-hearted, but very affectionate. With strong sex instincts he had only a child's control over them, and society had allowed them at first scant, then sudden, opportunities. Little girls are always apt to be the victims of sub-humans such as Cherry and such ignorance as Dominia's. Properly trained and treated, the Cherries could be made quite useful, and such revolting and preventable crimes removed from the list of our communal responsibilities.

Herded with men much worse than himself, Cherry, so manifestly a 'softy', for a time suffered the fate which nature seems to hold in store for the maimed; he suffered, physically, emotionally and morally. But help was at hand. There came into that gang a prisoner, one *Marcus*, esteemed incorrigible, 'in' for robbery with violence; and Marcus saw and understood! Then was the capacity for 'violence' vindicated, for Marcus, all unexpectedly, stood up for Cherry, and Cherry, in his turn, revealed another side of his nature, by his intense gratitude. It was years afterwards, when Cherry was 'out' and Marcus still 'in,' that I heard the story from Cherry, with whom there was no forgetting, and whose main anxiety now was to help his benefactor. With the Tims and Ninas, sound of wit but immature of heart, one does not find this faithfulness and gratitude—with them it's easy-come and easy-go, lose-one-friend-find-another, what's-the-odds! The angels, I think, are far nearer to Cherry & Co.; though how I wish they would guard them better, for these poor things are so dreadfully undiscriminating! Any hand, if only it is held out, will they gladly cling to, whether it be clean or dirty, whether it lead up or down. 'Do anything you told him, he would,' his own father says about Berry, another poor feeble-minded lad, who so far, has not come to gaol, only because he has a family to guard him. At the time we met he had just damaged some property with the utmost readiness, at the naughty behest of a boy-pal—strong-minded enough himself to 'stand-from-under.'

In the same way, even in prison, Cherry was employed to nefarious ends by one Clarence. Cherry, of course, did not see the game, or the true nature of his doings, still less that he was, in fact, cheating thereby, friends much more true. *Clarence*, who will be displaying himself in these pages a little further on, was a very clever young man, 'in' for 'false pretences,' but genuinely interested in motor-cars. Finding that Cherry was in touch with some nice kind folk who had resources which might haply be 'touched' through the 'softy,' Clarence persuaded his dupe to be 'interested in Motor-cars' also, and 'please could he have some books on them? A mate had told him such and such was a good one.' Delighted at having hit upon so 'constructive' a taste, and knowing nothing at the time of Cherry's real capacities, one friend did, accordingly, from time to time, supply some motor litera-ture which was quite expensive. Clarence enjoyed it greatly—while upon 'Cherry' its effect was magical! 'It is wonderful how his letters have improved!' remarked my innocent friend, not knowing that Clarence was kindly dictating them, for the spelling and writing were still poor Cherry's very own contribution. I believe that hopes had even begun to be entertained of 'genius allied to feeble-mindedness' in our poor lad, when, as usual, Clarence carelessly 'gave the show away.' It happened that, at the time I was given the letters of Cherry to my friend, I was corresponding with Clarence myself. A certain mannerism of style, peculiar to my correspondent, reappeared so often in those 'Cherry' letters that one would have been a fool not to make inquiry; and this drew the truth from the defaulter. Clarence, who, by this device, was not only getting together quite a useful little library but was also keeping his hand in at his usual crime, was greatly disgusted at the exposure. Poor bewildered Cherry, who had not intended the least harm but only wanted to oblige a 'friend,' was very unhappy at learning that he had done something unkind to his better friends. Very miserable, he wrote: 'I wish I did not have to be with these mans—they tell me what to do and I do it and its wrong.'

And that kind of thing, of course, is even more likely to happen when 'they' meet their easy dupe on release.

*Apple's* story is even sadder, because Apple is a girl; and a more good-hearted girl, Miss M. tells me, she has rarely met. She was 'adopted' as a baby and has a wretched tale to tell of cruelty at the hands of foster-parents, who, to do them justice, probably did not know that they had to do with a feeble mind, set, as it was, in a very good strong body. At the age of sixteen she ran away from 'home' to the nearest city, and there became a waitress at a night restaurant. In the case of a 'soft,' friendless, well-grown girl, the rest can readily be imagined. In wiser countries her status would have been ascertained in childhood, she would have been sheltered and trained, and happiness could have come to her. Dominia neither protected her, nor the public health through her, and presently something queer happened. The men who had been so eager for her company, particularly as she never had the wit to charge for it, 'wouldn't have her any longer,' and they told the Police. So she had to go to prison, and Hospital—and finally to a Mental Hospital. The men themselves, responsible though they were for this poor child's infection and ruin, were, of course, never brought to book. Such is Justice in Dominia (and elsewhere), and such our odd way of 'protecting the public.' Half Dominia's women prisoners, Miss M. tells me, are touched with the same mental defect.

*Snowy* is rather nearer to the normal than Cherry and Apple; though possibly the principal evidence of that fact is to be found in the childish cunning which is so often the pitiful weapon of the 'mentally inferior' aware of his handicap. In the absence of any scientific help, Dominia, of course, persists in regarding him as quite normal, and he was serving a long term for 'a little stealing,' when he began to write to me. Snowy loves to write letters, and 'I can assure you,' he says, 'that when I do get out I shan't be ashamed to write to you at any time.' He generally begins, 'News in Haste,' and goes on to say that there isn't any news. From the general muddle he makes of his affairs while in durance, it is not difficult to assess the state of his judgment, and his ability to compete on equal terms 'with his fellows.' He will begin a letter to a kinswoman 'Dear Sister,' and sign it 'Your affectionate uncle,' in defiance of human relationship. He will besiege one firm after another for work years before he has the least chance of release; and he openly cadges from anyone likely to take the least interest in him. Egotism is far more marked in *Snowy* than in such as *Cherry* and *Apple*, and so is ability, for he has a good manual training, and, with a guardian to direct his morals, he could easily earn his living. He would gladly accept a guardian, too, if Dominia only had the wit to give him one. 'I should be glad,' he writes, 'if at any time you would humbly send me a few words, and correct me about anything wrong, as it would be the means of showing and learning and giving me some good advice, and remember by so doing you are not offending in the least.'

Like Cherry, Snowy, too, would 'be a good boy if he could'; but he has learned how to render the aspiration in the true prison whine, with variations, thus:—

'After all is said and done, I have come to the conclusion that this going on in life is not worth the candle.'

Again: 'I am pleased to say that my enforced stay here in this institution 'as been the means of awakening within me all those better parts of my nature that I had allowed to become dormant, they at last predominate—after all I realise that this wrong-doing is not worth the candle.'

Again: another typical effort which this time concerns my letters. 'These,' he says, ''as been the means of uplifting me during my enforced stay in this institution. By the way, you asked me in your last letter to let you know where I am getting my big words from, reason is as follows: I find when I caroose certain passages in a book that appeals to me I try to conserstrate the same to my memory, because these passages help to uplift me and give me strength and hope to assist and cultivate all those good parts of my nature that I had for some time past allow to become dormant but which have now been awakened and thank God was now predominating.'

If Snowy spends much more time in prison, I have no doubt he will be able to copy still more long words out of a book, and spread the same sentiment over an entire page. Words seem to have a wonderful charm for him and his like. Witness Pearly! But Pearly deserves a chapter to himself.

Fools? Of course these are fools. But is not that community still more fond and foolish, and incalculably more criminal, which, giving no help to their pitiful helplessness, permits them first to drift into crime, and then, by forcing them to consort with criminals, degrades and ruins them still more? But, of course, these unfortunates are only somebody else's children.